Geff

The Unknown

Even the book morphs!
Flip the pages
and check it out!

Look for other **ANIMORPHS**™
titles by K.A. Applegate:

#1 The Invasion
#2 The Visitor
#3 The Encounter
#4 The Message
#5 The Predator
#6 The Capture
#7 The Stranger
#8 The Alien
#9 The Secret
#10 The Android
#11 The Forgotten
#12 The Reaction
#13 The Change

\<MEGAMORPHS\>
#1 The Andalite's Gift

ANIMORPHS™

The Unknown

K.A. Applegate

AN
APPLE
PAPERBACK

SCHOLASTIC INC.
New York Toronto London Auckland Sydney

For Michael and Jake

Cover illustration by David B. Mattingly

ISBN 0-590-49423-6

12 11 10 9 8 7 6 5 4 3 2 1   8 9/9 0 1/2 3/0

Printed in the U.S.A.   40

First Scholastic printing, January 1998

CHAPTER 1

My name is Cassie.

I can't tell you my last name. The Yeerk danger is too great. There are days when it feels like a noose slowly tightening around my neck. There are days when I don't feel like I can trust anyone. But as long as they don't know for sure who I am, maybe my friends and I can stay alive. Maybe.

Kind of dramatic-sounding, right? I sound like maybe I'm paranoid or nuts, don't I? Well, trust me, I'm not being overdramatic. I'm probably the least dramatic person you'll ever meet. And I'm not one of those crazy conspiracy people or anything. Really.

I'm just an average girl. I'm not some supermodel or rock star or whatever. I'm short. Okay-looking, but definitely not beautiful. I'm more stocky and solid than tall and willowy. If you want tall and willowy, you'll have to meet my best friend, Rachel.

But that's not me. I'm a short girl with short black hair and no makeup and a wardrobe that runs the gamut from jeans all the way to overalls. I own two pairs of boots. Both are currently covered with mud and various kinds of animal poop. I also have a couple of nice pairs of rubber gloves. You don't even want to know what's all over them.

See, I work with animals a lot. I help my dad, who's a veterinarian. He runs the Wildlife Rehabilitation Clinic, which is actually just our barn. He takes in all kinds of injured wildlife and sets their broken legs, and heals their mange, and soothes their burns, and disinfects their bites.

I help him out after school and on weekends. Mostly I do things like give the animals their "meds" — that's medications. I wash the animals and their cages, and feed them, and change dressings, and help my dad out in surgery. He's teaching me how to suture. You know — how to make stitches after you perform surgery.

Cool, huh? At least, to me it is. But in any case, now you know why I own poopy boots and gross gloves and several pairs of torn, stained jeans.

What can I say? I will not be appearing on the cover of *Seventeen*.

On the other hand, Rachel is my best friend, and Rachel is without a doubt the coolest person I will ever know. And Jake likes me — as in *likes* — and he's the smartest, strongest, most balanced person I've ever met. Except maybe for my parents, who are cool but in a parental way.

So anyway, I guess the lack of a decent wardrobe hasn't set me back too much. One way you can judge a person is by looking at their friends . . . and their enemies. I have wonderful friends.

And terrible enemies.

I have the kind of enemies that no normal, short, fashion-impaired animal nut should have.

Earth is being invaded. It is being invaded by a species of intelligent parasites called Yeerks. In their normal state they're just these grayish slugs. Like big fat snails without their shells. But the Yeerks have the ability to enter the brain of another animal, wrap themselves around the brain, sink into all the little cracks and crevices, and utterly take over.

The Yeerks have already enslaved the entire Hork-Bajir race. They've made allies of the vile Taxxons. And now they are after us.

They're here. They're all around you. You just don't know it. They can be anyone. You think you know your friends? Your teachers? Even your parents? Maybe you do. But maybe you don't. Because any of them might have a Yeerk living inside their head. Any one of them might be a Controller.

That's what we call a person who is enslaved by a Yeerk. A Controller. A human-Controller, which is a human who is completely enslaved by the Yeerk in his or her head.

I mentioned Jake earlier. His brother, Tom, is one of them. At school, our assistant principal, Chapman, is one of them.

And who is fighting to stop this invisible, secret Yeerk invasion? Just a bunch of kids. Jake, Rachel, Marco, Tobias, an alien kid named Ax, and yours truly.

Now you're worried. You're thinking, *Earth is being invaded by evil slugs from outer space and all we have on our side is a bunch of kids?*

Well, we're not exactly *just* a bunch of kids. We have certain abilities. See, we learned about the Yeerks from the dying Andalite prince, Elfangor. He gave us the Andalite morphing technology. It allows us to become any animal we can touch.

I've been a wolf and an osprey and a fly. I've been more than a dozen animals. I've been through terrible dangers, and awful, violent battles. But I'm still alive. Still just Cassie.

And I still don't care about clothes. Which just drives Rachel nuts, even after all these years.

Rachel was standing there in the barn, just staring at me.

"Cassie, I'm just saying, look, wear jeans if you want. Wear overalls. Wear crusty rubber boots. I can accept all that. But you could at least buy jeans that fit."

"These fit fine," I protested.

"Cassie, you know I love you. You know you're my best friend in the whole world. But those jeans are so short you could wade across the Mississippi and not get them wet. When did you buy them? When you were four?"

I looked down at my jeans. They did happen to end about an inch above the tops of my boots. I grinned at Rachel. She gets so distressed about things like that. There was a look of actual pain on her face. Like the mere existence of jeans this short was agonizing. "You're saying these are too short?"

"Not if there's a flood coming," Rachel said. "If you're expecting a flood, those would be the exact jeans to wear. Just come with me. I'm going to . . . the place. They're having lots of sales. I want you to come with me."

I narrowed my eyes. I knew what "the place" was. "I'm not going to the mall with you," I said.

5

"Who's going to the mall?" a voice asked.

It was my dad. He'd just opened the side door of the barn.

"Rachel is going to the mall," I told him.

"Please make her go with me," Rachel begged my father.

He laughed. "Nope. Sorry, Rachel. I need Cassie. Crazy Helen called and we have a sick horse way out on the edge of the Dry Lands."

Rachel looked down at my father's own jeans. They ended about six inches above his shoes, revealing socks that didn't exactly match.

"Gee, I wonder where Cassie gets it from?" Rachel said dryly.

I made a helpless shrug for Rachel. "Darn. Now I can't drag behind you for three hours while you power-shop and guys drool all over you. Oh, what a pity. Oh, life is so cruel."

Rachel made a face at me, then laughed. "Hey, a sick horse is far more important than buying jeans that go all the way down."

"Come with us," I said to Rachel. I like my dad and all, I really do, but a two-hour drive with just him and his old Stevie Wonder CD's was not going to be fun.

"Yeah, right," Rachel said.

I said, "Come with us, and tomorrow I'll let you pick out a new pair of jeans for me."

"*Real* jeans? Not some pair of blue cardboard-looking bargain jeans?" Rachel bit her lip, and got a misty look in her eyes. "Of course, you'll need a nice top to go with them. . . ."

And that's how we ended up discovering the evil horses that threatened all of humanity.

But I'd better not get ahead of myself. First we had to drive to the Dry Lands.

CHAPTER 2

It was dark by the time we got away from the city, away from the far edge of forest and out into the area we usually called the Dry Lands.

The Dry Lands aren't exactly desert. I mean, we're not talking cactuses and so on. But the area is a kind of wasteland of scruffy grass and lots of emptiness that seems to stretch on and on forever. Here and there you'll see a tree, or maybe a few trees, but mostly it's all just grass and wildflowers and scrub and piles of boulders that jut up out of the ground like they were piled there by some ancient giant.

Not that we saw much of the Dry Lands that night. It was highway all the way there. An hour of highway, with all three of us crammed in the front seat of the pickup. My dad won't let us ride in the back. It's not safe.

But of course Rachel and I couldn't really talk much, with my dad right there. It's not just that he's a parent. It's also that he doesn't know anything about our lives as Animorphs.

"So, who's Crazy Helen?" Rachel asked, desperate for anything to talk about.

"Probably shouldn't call her that," my dad said. "Even though that's what she calls herself. She's an old woman, maybe eighty years old. She has a trailer behind a souvenir shop she owns. I met her years back when there was trouble with the Dry Lands horse herds."

"There was a problem with intestinal parasites," I explained. "Worms."

"For who? The horses or Crazy Helen?" Rachel asked.

"There it is," my dad said, interrupting my search for a really funny comeback to Rachel.

He pulled the truck up to a souvenir stand topped by a gigantic billboard that read LAST CHANCE SOUVENIRS. The billboard was bigger than the actual store. The store was closed and looked like it had been for years.

Behind the store was a trailer. It was an Airstream. You know, one of those silver, bullet-shaped trailers? There was an awning out front trimmed in bright Christmas lights. Even though it was nowhere near Christmas.

Crazy Helen came out when she saw us pull up. She had stringy gray hair and was wearing a faded flowery blouse over patched jeans and cowboy boots.

"Hey," Rachel said. "It's *you,* Cassie. In sixty or seventy years."

I "accidentally" dug my elbow into Rachel's side, and we both laughed.

"Actually, Cassie, you'll end up running some big volunteer organization that saves unhappy chickens and whales or whatever," Rachel said, softening her sarcasm.

I kind of liked that picture of my future. Although I wasn't sure how I was going to work with chickens and whales at the same time.

"She's over there. Over *there,*" Crazy Helen yelled as soon as we piled out of the truck. "It's a big roan mare. She's acting all funny. Like maybe she's been eating the loco weed."

"Loco weed?" Rachel asked me.

I shrugged.

"Hi, Helen," my dad said calmly. "We'll go take a look, see what we have. How have you been?"

"Those darn aliens still won't let me sleep," she said.

I saw Rachel stiffen. I gave her a wink. In a low whisper I said, "Different aliens."

"They keep sending me the messages through my teeth," Helen said. "They keep on telling me they're gonna land, right out here. But I haven't seen a Martian land in forty years. Very untrustworthy. Very, very sneaky, untrustworthy folks."

"Who?" my father asked.

"The Martians, that's who." Crazy Helen laughed. It wasn't an insane laugh. More of a gentle, knowing sound. I wondered sometimes if Crazy Helen was really crazy, or just playing a game.

"Well, we'll go look at this horse," my dad said.

Rachel and I shone flashlights into the dark. The moon was up, but it was just a sliver and didn't cast much light. And soon we were beyond the pool of light from the trailer and the billboard. Out in the absolute blackness you get when you're far from the city.

The flashlight picked out stumpy trees and bushes and rocks. The only sound was the rustling of the tall grass as we walked.

My father and I peered deep into the gloom, looking for a horse. Rachel, on the other hand, turned to look back toward the highway.

"Hey. Is that the horse you're looking for?" Rachel asked.

"Where?"

"There. Back by the road. Back by that pay phone."

My dad and I turned back to look. A scruffy roan horse was swaying from side to side as it walked. Swaying like a drunk.

As we watched, the horse seemed to be attracted to the telephone. It picked up the receiver with its mouth and let it hang off the hook.

And that's when things got strange. The horse lowered its head to the ground, picked up a twig in its lips, and seemed to be poking the telephone keyboard.

"Am I crazy, or is that horse trying to make a phone call?" Rachel said.

My dad shrugged. "Must be disoriented. Doesn't know what it's doing. Come on, let's get over there."

I dropped behind a few steps to fall in with Rachel.

"That horse is dialing the phone," Rachel said in a whisper.

"Sure looks like it," I agreed.

"Ordering a pizza?" Rachel suggested.

"Hay, alfalfa, and extra cheese?"

My dad was getting close to the horse. The horse spotted him, and hesitated. Like it wanted to complete its phone call. But also wanted to run away. It decided to run. Only it wasn't really up for running. The best it could do was wobble off into the darkness, practically falling over as it went.

"Whoa, girl, whoa," my dad said in his calming-the-animals voice. "Whoa. I'm just trying to help you."

But the horse wasn't interested. It swayed and wobbled and drifted away as fast as it could. I lost it in the darkness, but then we heard a WHUMPF sound.

I broke into a run and soon caught up to my father. He was kneeling over the fallen horse. The horse was still trying to stand up, but it was out of it.

"What do you think it is?" I asked my dad anxiously. The horse was sweating profusely. It glared at us with huge brown eyes.

"Well, it could be a lot of things," he answered. "But I'd put my money on snake bite. Try and keep her calm. I have to get some things from the truck. I'll be right back."

"Snakes?" Rachel said.

"Sure. There are lots of snakes out here," I said. I patted the horse's flank and made soothing noises.

"Not at night, though, right? I mean, snakes are probably a daytime thing . . . right?"

"Not always."

"Great. This is much better than the mall. Poison snakes and phone-calling horses."

Suddenly I noticed something happening to the horse's head. "Look!" I cried.

There, crawling its way out of the horse's left ear, was a slug. A large gray slug.

"Is that what I think it is?" Rachel whispered.

"Yeah. I think so."

The gray slug wormed its way out of the horse's head. It plopped heavily on the gravel and grass beneath it. And then it started to writhe away.

I'd seen those slugs before. We both had.

"Yeerk," I whispered. "There was a Yeerk in this horse."

The Yeerk crawled into the darkness. I glanced back and saw my dad still digging through his medical supplies at the truck. And that's when the pale stallion appeared.

He was not a terribly large horse. But you knew right away, from the first glance, that this was a powerful animal. He stepped calmly toward us, head held high. He looked down at the snake-bit horse. And then he looked at the crawling Yeerk.

It was hard to see clearly in the dark, but I think the Yeerk tried to raise itself up to the horse. Like it was trying to reach it. Then the stallion turned and began to run away.

"Rachel?"

"Yeah."

"We have to get out of here."

"What do you mean? Why?"

I didn't know why. It was a feeling. An instinct. But it was really strong. "Just do it. Run! RUN!"

I grabbed Rachel's arm and yanked her along with me. We took about eight steps, then . . .

TSSEEEEEWWW! TSSEEEEEWWW!

A blinding light! Brilliant and intense as a flashbulb-in-your-face light! The light was coming from above. From the sky.

The very rocks split open. The ground itself seeming to explode!

My face hit the dirt before I even knew I was falling.

CHAPTER 3

I was on my back. I was indoors. I opened my eyes. Staring down at me was an alien. A pale, ghostly oval face with two enormous eyes. It looked like a little kid, with weak arms and legs.

It looked like one of the aliens from that old movie, *Close Encounters of the Third Kind*. In fact, it looked *exactly* like one of them.

I blinked and looked again. It was a life-size cardboard cutout. Standing just behind the alien was Data from *Star Trek: The Next Generation*.

I sat up. All around me were shelves piled with *Star Wars* masks — Wookiees and Darth Vader and Imperial stormtroopers, along with

Star Trek handheld phasers and Spock ears. There were posters everywhere — Mulder and Scully from *X-Files,* Mike, Crow, Servo, and Gypsy from *Mystery Science Theater 3000,* Jane Fonda as Barbarella, and movie posters from *Plan 9 From Outer Space, The Day the Earth Stood Still, Invasion of thc Body Snatchers* and, of course, *2001: A Space Odyssey.*

But mostly there were posters, mugs, ashtrays, pencils, and T-shirts, all emblazoned with a red-and-white logo dominated by the stencil letters spelling "Zone: 91."

"She's awake," Rachel said. She sauntered over, carrying a short stick in one hand.

"What's going on?" I asked her.

"You were knocked out. You know, when that totally unexplainable explosion happened." She arched one brow and gave me a meaningful look.

I understood. Rachel was reminding me that we had not seen what we had seen — there had been no Yeerk crawling from a horse's ear. There had been no Dracon beam.

My father came rushing over, followed by Crazy Helen. He knelt and began feeling my head.

"Ow!"

"Looks okay," he muttered. "Superficial cut. Serious bruise, but I doubt there's a concussion.

Still, I'll take you by the hospital emergency room on the way home. Have the doctors there check you out."

Rachel winked. "Doctor Carter may be there. Noah Wyle. Oh, *yeah*."

"What happened?" I asked my dad.

"Well, honey —"

"It was the aliens," Crazy Helen interrupted. "They have these exploding rocks they spread around out there. BOOM!"

My father rolled his eyes. "We're on the edge of an Air Force facility. They have a base way back in the Dry Lands. You see the jets flying over all the time. I suspect they may have lost a bomb or a missile or something. That snake-bit horse must have set it off. The blast caught you."

"That sounds logical," I said.

"It was the aliens!" Crazy Helen screamed. "They keep the aliens out at Zone Ninety-one! That's why it's all so secret out there. That's why the Air Force won't talk about it. Zone Ninety-one is the secret base where the government keeps the aliens it has captured. They have 'em out there in cages. They get secrets of technology from them. You think computers just happened? All that stuff was from aliens. Here, have a sou-venir mug. Normally ten-ninety-nine. But you can have it because you got hurt."

Helen grabbed a mug from the shelf, wiped it off on her sleeve, and handed it to me.

Rachel held up her stick. "I got a pecan log," she said.

"You want a mug?" Helen asked her.

"No, the pecan log is great. But I don't really believe in aliens." Rachel said this with a perfectly straight face.

Helen just smiled. "Lots of people *do,* young lady. Very smart people, too. Out at Zone Ninety-one they know. Oh, *they* know! The government doesn't want us telling. They watch me. They listen in through the microchip they implanted in my head. They're listening right now! One of those black helicopters of theirs is listening in and transmitting everything we say to the New World Order headquarters in the Azores, which is where Atlantis is, you know."

This tirade left us all temporarily without anything much to say. We just kind of stared.

"Well, we may as well get out of Helen's hair," my father said, breaking the spell. "Cassie, honey, do you feel okay? Can you focus your eyes?"

"Um, yes," I said. "But how about that horse?"

My father shook his head, mystified. "Strangest thing. There isn't a trace left of her. Not a trace."

"Hah. It's the Martians," Crazy Helen said. "It's all the fault of those darned aliens."

Rachel and I exchanged a look. We were both having the same thought: *It's a very strange world where a person called Crazy Helen is at least partly right.*

CHAPTER 4

"You've never heard of Zone Ninety-one before? It's the Holy Grail of conspiracy nuts," Marco said in between slurps of a Mountain Dew. "Man, don't you ever go on the Internet? The Internet is full of people who think there are aliens at Zone Ninety-one. It's called the Most Secret Place On Earth."

"I go on the Internet," Rachel said. "I just don't hang out in chat rooms, call myself 'Studboy,' and try to convince people I'm an incredibly handsome thirty-year-old millionaire."

"Excuse me," Marco said, "but I do not use 'Studboy' as my screen name. Give me some credit. I use BaldwinBoyFive. You know, the missing fifth Baldwin brother. The really cool-looking one."

We were all at the mall food court, the day after the incident in the Dry Lands. I was clutching a shopping bag. Inside were several smaller bags from The Gap and J. Crew.

It was all Rachel's doing. Despite everything, she had actually remembered my stupid promise. Now I owned outfits. Not just clothing, mind you. *Outfits*.

"Even I've heard of Zone Ninety-one," Jake said. "And unlike Marco, I'm a fairly normal human being."

Marco threw a french fry at Jake. Jake ducked. And with a quick movement, Ax snagged the french fry out of midair, popped it in his mouth and said, "Mmmm. Grease. Greassss and salt!"

Just then a boy walked up to the table. He seemed nervous, edgy. Like he was a little scared by the experience of being in the mall. He looked over his shoulders a lot. And when he looked right at you he squinted, as if he was near-sighted.

"Hey, Tobias," Marco said. "We were thinking about ordering some pizza. You want mouse meat on yours?"

Maybe I should back up a little and explain

who all these people are. Because otherwise you'd never guess that this bunch was the Animorphs.

First, there's Jake. Jake is pretty much the leader. Not that anyone really treats him that way. And not that he'd want anyone to treat him that way. See, that's part of the reason Jake *is* our leader — because he's the kind of guy who doesn't need anyone sucking up to him.

Then there's Marco. What can I say about Marco? Not as much as he would say about himself, that's for sure.

Marco is our sense of humor in the group. But he is not the class clown. There's a seriousness to him, way down beneath all the glib jokes and teasing. Marco sees things other people sometimes miss. He is very smart and very wide-awake, if you know what I mean.

Marco is Jake's best friend. They've been best friends forever. No one even remembers when it started. But ever since their friendship began, they've been arguing with each other about the most completely idiotic things in the universe: whether you should use more pedal or higher gears to win this dumb driving video game they love; whether Spiderman could beat Batman; whether basketball takes more teamwork than football; whether cheese tastes yellow.

I'm *not* kidding. They once spent an entire Saturday arguing whether something could taste like a color. I seem to remember that Marco thought cheese actually tasted green.

Despite this, Jake and Marco, along with Rachel and me, are the most normal members of the Animorphs. The other two are definitely weirder.

Take Tobias. Tobias is a kid trapped in the body of a red-tailed hawk. That happens if you stay more than two hours in a morph. You stay in that morph permanently. Tobias lives in the forest near a meadow. He still lives by hunting mice and rabbits.

But a vastly powerful creature called an El-limist just recently gave Tobias back his power to morph. So now Tobias can morph like any of us. Except that just as we each have to return to our human form before two hours, Tobias has to return to his hawk form.

So the human body Tobias was in at the mall was actually a morph of his old human body. That's why he seemed nearsighted: He was used to his laser-sharp hawk eyes.

He could stay forever in that human body, but then he'd be trapped as a human, unable to morph.

Confusing? It gets worse.

The last member of our group is not a human at all. His full name is Aximili-Esgarrouth-Isthill. We call him Ax.

Ax is an Andalite. But he also has a human morph he created out of bits of DNA from Jake, Marco, me, and Rachel.

Ax in his human morph is shockingly pretty for a boy. And extremely weird. See, Andalites have no mouths. No sense of taste. So when Ax is in human morph and has a mouth, he has no resistance whatsoever to flavors.

Ax is dangerous around cinnamon buns. And chocolate. And popcorn. And the paper boxes the popcorn comes in.

Basically, Ax in human morph should not go anywhere near anything that can be eaten. We've had to stop him from eating the butts out of ashtrays. Don't get me wrong. Ax is brilliant and decent and honorable and brave — when he's in his own body.

"So. What's up?" Tobias asked.

Six sets of eyes casually scanned the area around us. The mall was not busy, and it was too early for a big dinner crowd at the food court. But we had to be sure that no one was even slightly within range to overhear.

Our enemies could be any*one*. Any*where*.

"Rachel and Cassie went out to Zone Ninety-one and found horses making phone calls," Marco said.

Tobias's eyes darted to me, then to Rachel. He looked very serious. He had mostly forgotten how to make human expressions with his face. But he was still Tobias. "Can someone interpret from Marco-babble to normal language?"

"I think I like you better as a chicken, Tobias," Marco said.

"Red-tailed hawk," Tobias said tolerantly.

Marco shrugged. "Chicken, pigeon, hawk, whatever."

"Um, how about if we get down to business before someone interrupts us?" Jake suggested.

"Okay, *Dad*," Marco said. Then, becoming instantly serious, he quickly and efficiently summarized for Tobias what we knew.

"Yeerks in horses," Rachel said. "It makes zero sense. Why would Yeerks want to make Controllers out of horses?"

"Do horses have some special powers? Powwerz-zuh?" Ax asked. In addition to enjoying taste, he finds speaking words out loud to be strange.

I shrugged. "They're herd animals. Not very smart. In fact, pretty dumb, really. They can run fast, but there are lots of faster animals. They're strong, but there are lots of other animals that are stronger." I shrugged again. "I can't see why the Yeerks would be wanting to infest horses."

"Maybe they think they can win the Kentucky Derby," Rachel joked.

"Maybe it's some kind of strange Yeerk entertainment," Jake offered. "Maybe it's fun for them."

"I don't believe Yeerks do anything for fun, Prince Jake," Ax said. "They would have some reason."

"Ax, please don't call me 'Prince Jake.' Especially not in public."

"Yes, Prince Jake. Jay-kuh."

"Are you two sure about this?" Jake asked Rachel and me. "It was a Yeerk you saw? Not a snake or a snail or something?"

"And what if your dad is right, and it was an exploding artillery shell, not a Dracon flash?" Tobias suggested.

"We're not doubting you," Jake added quickly. "It's just that there's no good reason for Yeerks to infest horses."

I looked at Rachel. I was sure of what we'd seen. Mostly. "Well . . . I guess I could be wrong. But I'm pretty sure."

"Yeah. Pretty sure," Rachel echoed.

"So? What do we do?" Jake asked. "Take a look around out in the Dry Lands? See if we can get some more proof?"

"Very good flying out there," Tobias said. "Lots of sweet thermals."

"And plenty of delicious snakes and toads?" Marco asked with mock innocence.

"I can't go tomorrow," Jake said. "It's my dad's birthday. We're all going out for dinner."

"Even Tom?" Rachel asked.

"Tom says he'll be there," Jake said darkly. "But who knows? He spends a lot of time at meetings of The Sharing lately. All the more reason why I *have* to be there. My dad is not going to celebrate his birthday without at least one of his sons there."

"What did you get your dad?" I asked, trying to lighten the mood.

Jake grinned. "Haven't done it yet, but I think I'm going to clean the roof gutters for him."

Marco shuddered. "Actual physical labor? Couldn't you just get him a nice Hallmark card?"

"I am kind of curious about this thing with the horses," I said. "But we could put it off till the weekend."

"It could be worth checking out," Jake said. "But we don't need everyone to go along. Who wants to go flying with Cassie tomorrow after school?"

In the end Tobias, Rachel, Marco, and I decided to go. Jake was busy, and I don't think Ax saw any point in it. We broke up and went our separate ways. We try not to spend much time together in public. We don't want any inquisitive Controllers to start thinking of us as a "group." So Rachel and I left together.

"No one is taking this seriously, are they?" I asked her. "I get the impression Ax thinks we're nuts."

"Yeerks in horses? Horse-Controllers? It is kind of hard to see where that's some big threat."

"Yeah. I guess that's true."

"But hey, any excuse to go flying, right?"

CHAPTER 5

The next day I wore my new outfit to school. I hooked up with Rachel before first period and we walked to class together. Down the main hall. Me and Rachel, the Goddess of Clothing and Good Grooming.

"You look great!" Rachel said.

"Hi, Rachel," a boy named Charles said, smiling awkwardly. "Oh, and hi, um . . . Carla."

"See? Charles smiled at you."

"He called me *Carla.*"

"Has he ever even spoken to you before?" Rachel asked.

"I guess not."

"See? Progress."

Marco likes to tease Rachel, calling her Xena: Warrior Princess. And when I'm with her I guess I'm Gabrielle. The sidekick. Guys see Rachel first, second, and third. They see me fourth.

Personally, I don't care. Looks and clothing don't matter even slightly to me. And the people who matter are the ones who see past all that.

"Hey, Rachel. How's it going?" a boy named Jawan asked, smiling shyly.

"Fine," Rachel said coolly. "Cassie, you've met Jawan, haven't you?"

I shrugged. "Hi, Jawan."

"Hey, Kendra," he said. "See you later in English, Rachel."

"*Kendra*?" I asked Rachel.

"He gave you a definite look," Rachel said. "So what if he isn't good at remembering names?"

"He remembers *your* name pretty well," I pointed out. Then I spotted a guy named Joe. Joe was a friend of mine from when we both took riding lessons together. He would remember my name.

"Hey, Cassie. Whoa! Whoa! Something different about you." He stepped back and stared at me.

"New outfit?" Rachel suggested.

Joe shook his head. "No, that's not it. Oh, I

know what it is!" He snapped his fingers. "You look like you've gained weight! Have you been trying to bulk up?"

Rachel reached with one elegant hand and pushed Joe disdainfully out of her way.

"That proves nothing," Rachel said.

"Uh-huh. I look fatter."

"Guys are idiots sometimes."

"Not Jake," I said.

Rachel rolled her eyes. "Jake is the exception that proves the rule," she said. "And there he is now."

Jake was cruising down the hall, joking and talking with some non-Animorph friends. Part of what we have to do is maintain normal lives as much as possible.

"Hi, Cassie," Jake said, peeling off from his buds. "Hey, Rachel."

Rachel stood back, and held her hands out toward me like a fashion designer showing off her latest supermodel. "So?"

"So what?" Jake asked blankly.

"So the outfit! The outfit!" Rachel exploded in frustration. "Doesn't Cassie look great in these new clothes? These clothes that actually fit, and have no raccoon poop stains? Doesn't she look fabulous?"

Jake smiled his slow smile. "Of course she looks great. She *always* does. You guys have fun in the Dry Lands this afternoon. And try to be careful."

He walked off down the hall leaving me with a nice, warm glow.

Rachel stared at me. "Okay, he's an idiot, too."

"No, you were right the first time," I said smugly. "He's the exception."

We reached first period class. I sighed deeply, my usual reaction to first period. The classroom was stuffy and airless. The windows just looked out at the blank brick wall of the gym.

I went to my seat and tried to remind myself of what we were supposed to have studied the night before. Did I do my homework? Oh, yeah. I had. It was in my —

"No! No! It can't be!"

Marco's voice. He sits two rows over. But now he leaped clear over one row of seats and slithered into an empty desk next to mine. He stared at me, wide-eyed with wonder. Way too much wonder.

"Who is this vision of loveliness? Who is this fantasy come true? Excuse me, but are you Tyra Banks? No, no, you can't be any mortal girl. So much perfection could never be achieved by a mere human. You're an angel descended from heaven! I mean, they say clothes make the man, but these clothes make you an *angel*."

I took out my homework and placed it on my desk. "Are you done?" I asked Marco.

He thought for a moment, then nodded. "Yeah. That should be about enough."

"What did Rachel pay you?"

He grinned. "Two bucks. Girls are such idiots sometimes. I'd have done it for a dollar."

CHAPTER 6

We met up at the Wildlife Rehabilitation Clinic.

I quickly doled out the meds to the caged patients. It was a slow week. Half the cages were empty, which is totally unusual.

"You ready?" Rachel asked.

"Just have to check this opossum's bandage. Good. The stitches are holding. Good boy," I said to the opossum with the mangled paw. "Okay. Now I'm ready."

"Why do they have that extra *o* in opossum?" Marco wondered. "What's the point of it if it's silent?"

Tobias was up in the rafters. He was in his hawk body once more. A red-tailed hawk with a brown back and tan front and reddish-brown tail. His eyes were gold and inhumanly intense.

Since he was in morph, he communicated in thought-speak. <Everything's clear,> he said to me. <Your mom just went inside the house carrying groceries. Your dad's truck is just coming through the intersection by the Exxon station. It'll take him five minutes to get here.>

I didn't doubt Tobias. Hawks have amazing vision. From his position in the rafters of the barn, Tobias could see out through the open loft door. If he said my dad was five minutes away, my dad was five minutes away.

"Let's morph," Rachel said.

She removed her outer clothing and folded it neatly into her backpack. Beneath she wore her morphing suit. See, we haven't figured out how to morph bulky clothing. We can only morph something fairly skintight. Like Rachel's black leotard. Or my somewhat more colorful aerobics outfit. Or Marco's bike shorts.

I focused my mind on the morph I wanted to do. It was an osprey, a type of hawk that usually eats fish and lives by water. It would be good for distance flying.

Rachel was morphing her own big bird of prey, a bald eagle. Marco has an osprey morph, just like mine. In fact, identical to mine, since we acquired the same bird's DNA.

I began to focus on the osprey, and as I did, I felt the changes begin.

Morphing is still exciting to me. I've done it dozens and dozens of times, but each time I realize how lucky I am to have the power. I will never get tired of it. I'll never get bored with it. It is an experience of total, complete, utterly amazing change.

Each morph happens differently. Things happen in unpredictable ways. It isn't always smooth and gradual. Often it's unbelievably illogical, and you never know quite what will happen first.

This time the first change I noticed was my legs. Without getting smaller, they began to morph into bird legs. My five small toes melted together. And from those melted toes grew long talons. Three long talons forward, one turned back.

Looking down, I could see why people say birds descended from dinosaurs. A hawk talon looks exactly like the foot of a Tyrannosaurus or some other big predator dinosaur.

A hawk talon is one of those things where you can just look at it and know it's a weapon. They're fleshless and without feathers, so that the blood of prey animals doesn't stick and turn nasty; they're quick and powerful at gripping, but weak and reluctant to let go; and the claw at the end is designed not just to hold a branch, or to walk on, but to be squeezed directly into the flesh of the prey.

Nature, as I learned from my parents, isn't always warm and cuddly.

"She's got le-egs, she knows how to use them." Marco sang the line of an old song. Then he laughed, but the laugh was cut short when his mouth erupted into an osprey's beak.

The next change was my skin. It lightened toward medium gray. And all across the skin of my arms I saw patterns being drawn. Feather patterns, like tiny trees pressed flat. Networks of tiny veins that overlapped like shingles on a roof.

Then, rippling across my body, the patterns became three-dimensional. The patterns seemed to swell up and become full-fledged feathers.

It itched. But it did not hurt. I resisted the urge to scratch. Because already my fingers were not exactly fingers anymore. The finger bones had begun to elongate. At the same time my arm bones contorted and shrank, becoming lighter, air-filled, hollow.

Bones make a sort of grinding sound when they morph. It's disturbing the first few times you do it. To put it mildly.

Finally, I began shrinking. The ground began to rush up toward me. Even though I've done this many times, I still can't quite shake the feeling that I'm falling and falling and falling without ever quite hitting bottom.

I had left my boots standing right near me. They're rubber boots that come up to about midcalf. But now, as I shrank, the boots grew. From midcalf height to waist height in less than a minute.

And I was still shrinking.

At the same time my internal organs began to shift and rearrange. My long, twisted human intestines became the much shorter digestive tract of a bird. My slow, plodding human heart became the rapid-fire heart of an osprey. Kidneys, lungs, liver . . . nothing stayed the same.

Then . . . SPRROOOT! My lips bulged out and out and very suddenly became harder than fingernails. I had a curved, ripping hawk's beak.

I felt my teeth sort of shrivel way I felt my forehead recede and my chest narrow. All the fat on my body disappeared, leaving me little more than skin and and muscle and hollow bones wrapped in feathers.

I noticed several of the animals in the cages watching us with great intensity. None more intense than an injured fox who seemed mesmerized by the way we had gone from being huge, threatening humans to small, tasty birds. He watched me with hungry, glittering eyes.

<Better get a move on,> Tobias said. <We should be well clear before Cassie's dad gets here.>

<Yeah,> Marco said. <We look like we're here to break into the cages and bust the other birds outta here.>

I spread my arms. But instead of arms I had wings. <I'm ready. Rachel?>

I looked at Rachel. Her human eyes were just changing color. She stared back at me with an eagle's intense gaze. <Ready.>

<Let's fly,> I said. I opened my wings and beat them downward, hard. And again. And again. I drew my talons up and beat several times more.

I rose from the floor of the barn. It was a struggle. We were inside, in a cramped area with no headwind.

I beat my wings and rose to the loft to perch beside Tobias. Rachel came to rest just across from us. She was nearly twice our size, with wings that stretched six feet from tip to tip and a blazingly white head and tail.

I looked out through the open hayloft. I looked with osprey eyes. It's as if humans are blind. I saw my dad's truck coming down the dirt road to our farm. I saw through the windshield. I saw his face. I saw the individual hairs on his head. If a fly had landed on his nose right then, I'd have been able to see its antennae twitch.

My dad was still two hundred yards away.

Then I lifted my gaze toward the rectangle of blue and white sky.

I opened my wings, launched myself forward, swooped out through the window, caught just enough of a breeze, and soared toward the clouds.

There are times when being an Animorph is pretty bad. But definitely not when you're flying.

CHAPTER 7

There is a lot to know about flying. Fortunately, the osprey's brain took care of most of that. It trimmed my tail. It adjusted the angle of my wings. But my brain was there, too. And I flew.

We flapped hard to get some altitude and rise above the barn and my house. In a few seconds we were high enough for me to spot the orange Frisbee I'd accidentally thrown onto the roof of my house. We circled, fighting gravity, and I could see my dad pulling his truck up to the mailbox to check for letters.

Higher still, and I could see through my own living room window and see my mom tilting her head back, eyes closed, relaxing after a day at work.

<This way,> Tobias called to us, and Rachel and I followed. The sky is home to Tobias. He knows his way around. Rachel and I are just visitors to the clouds.

<See over there? Off to the east?> Tobias asked. <See the way the clouds are piled up? The slight rippling in the air?>

I looked with my incredible osprey vision. And I did see the air ripple from heat. The same way you sometimes see heat waves rising from the pavement on a hot day. But these heat waves were half a mile away.

<Yes,> I replied. <I see them. Is it a thermal?>

<A serious thermal. We'll ride that a mile straight up!>

After all this time, Tobias is still excited by flying. I guess I would be, too. It is the coolest thing in the world.

We flew hard, separated by a few hundred yards so we wouldn't look like we were together. See, red-tails, bald eagles, and ospreys don't exactly fly in formation together.

I felt my wing muscles grow tired. Flapping is hard work. But when we reached the thermal it would be easier. A thermal is a pillar of rising warm air. You spread your wings in a thermal, and you can soar with very little energy.

Then, wonderfully, we were in it. I felt warm air billow up beneath my outstretched wings. And up I soared. Up and up and up!

<Hah-hah! Oh, man I love this!> Rachel yelled. <I love this, I love this, I love this! Yeeeee-haaah!>

<So, you're saying you love this?> Marco asked her.

Up we went, circling over and under and around each other. We were doing an airborne ballet of incredible gracefulness.

The ground fell away beneath us. Now even our excellent predators' hearing picked up no sound from the cars and houses and stores below us.

Up we went, till the tallest trees looked like tiny bushes. Till lawns became postage stamps. Till roads became shimmering streams of hot concrete.

And yet, even though everything below us became small, I could still see in startling detail. Especially anything that moved like prey: cats, dogs, mice, other birds.

<Look,> Tobias said. <A flight of geese!>

I saw them up above us. They were going the same direction as us, but moving in a tight V-formation.

<Let's go catch them!> I cried.

Tobias laughed. <Yeah, right. See the way they fly? They never stop flapping. They're like machines. They can fly hundreds of miles. You ever watch a dog try to catch a passing car? That's what it would be like, us trying to catch those geese.>

He was right. The geese just kept power-flying. Soon they were way past us.

<How long till we get to the Dry Lands?> Rachel asked.

<Long time,> Tobias said. <But we're getting some great altitude. That will help.>

<This will be so cool,> Marco said. <Zone Ninety-one! We will penetrate the very heart of the government conspiracy to cover up alien visitors!>

<Marco, just how dumb are you?> Rachel asked. <We know about the *real* aliens. We know they don't look like E.T. or the guys you always see on alien books. And we know the real aliens, the Yeerks, don't go around kidnapping backwoods goobers and doing medical experiments on them.>

<Maybe there are two different bunches of aliens,> Marco said. <Maybe there are these aliens who crash-landed back in the fifties. Plus the Yeerks more recently.>

<Yeah, right, Agent Mulder,> Rachel grumbled. <Earth is the crossroads of every passing

alien. We're the McDonald's next to the highway of the galaxy.>

They argued on for a while, and, not for the first time, I realized my life had gotten weird. I was flying a mile up, listening to a thought-speak debate between a bald eagle and an osprey over the existence of aliens.

Good grief.

After a while I tuned them out. It is very quiet in the high air. No noise from the ground. None. Sometimes you hear the engines of a jet flying by, five miles farther up. But mostly all you hear is the soft rushing of wind over feathers. And the sound of your own wings beating.

We used the altitude of the first thermal to jump from thermal to thermal. We would fly out of one gentle vortex of warm air, descend to the next, and let it raise us up again.

And after a while, I saw the roads becoming fewer and smaller. The houses thinned out. The gas stations were miles apart. I saw cows and sheep standing around in random patterns far below.

And then even the cows and sheep were left behind as were the last homes and businesses. Below us the ground was dry, covered with yellowed grass, and marked out by barbed-wire fences.

Tobias said, <Hey. Check out that sign down there. The one by the dirt road.>

I aimed my osprey vision and read:

STOP!

GOVERNMENT PROPERTY. RESTRICTED AREA.
AUTHORIZED PERSONNEL ONLY BEYOND THIS POINT.
ALL OTHERS ARE SUBJECT TO ARREST AND
PROSECUTION. THIS MEANS YOU.

<I'm guessing this is the beginning of the famous Zone Ninety-one,> I said.

<Friendly, aren't they?> Rachel said.

<If you were trying to conceal a vast government conspiracy to hide an alien spacecraft, you'd be paranoid, too,> Marco said.

I wasn't sure whether he was joking or not. Sometimes it's hard to tell with Marco.

I could see the base called Zone 91. It was a cluster of squat, unattractive buildings that all looked as if they'd been built forty years ago. There were three very large buildings that looked like aircraft hangars. And there was an airstrip. But I could also see lots of vehicles: trucks, Humvees, even some tanks.

And there were horses, just scattering, sauntering through the base like it wasn't there.

<Marco, I know a lady you'd love,> Rachel

muttered. <Her name is Crazy Helen. Crazy, because she sounds like you.>

<Let's look for those horses,> I suggested. <I think that's the place to start.>

<The phone-using horses,> Tobias said. <Horse-Controllers.>

Something about the way he said it made it sound like he doubted the whole thing.

<We *did* see a Yeerk crawl out of that horse's ear,> Rachel said defensively.

<And we *did* almost get fried by a Bug fighter's Dracon beam,> I pointed out.

<You didn't actually see a Bug fighter, though. And with pathetic human eyes, who can tell if it's a Yeerk slug or just a plain old snake? Now that I can become human again, I can really remember how blind humans are.>

<I cannot believe you don't believe us, Tobias,> Rachel complained.

<I didn't say I don't believe you. It's just that it doesn't make any sense. I mean, why would Yeerks want to infest some skanky wild horses?>

<I don't know,> I admitted. <But I know what I saw.>

<There!> Rachel said. <A bunch of horses. Over by the water hole. Maybe that's them.>

We banked sharply left and headed toward them. There were half a dozen mares, two gangly colts, and one big stallion who stood off by himself on a slight rise. The stallion sniffed the breeze, head high.

<That's not them,> I said.

<How do you know?>

<Because they're acting exactly like horses, that's why. They have colts. And the stallion is behaving like a stallion. The horses we want won't act that way.>

<Okay. Well, you guys need to demorph,> Tobias said. <You're nearly at the two-hour limit. There are some rocks over there. You'll have shade and privacy.>

So we headed for the rocks and landed. They were just a pile of rocks like any other jumble of boulders.

Except that we'd overlooked one vital fact: They were on the far side of the sign. The sign that said THIS MEANS YOU.

49

CHAPTER 8

We flew down into the rocks and demorphed.

It was a nice little enclosure, with tall, rounded boulders all around us and clean, dry sand under our feet. We were completely hidden from anyone coming in any direction.

Tobias came to rest beside us as Marco, Rachel, and I returned to our human forms. Of course, as always when we came out of a morph, we were in our morphing suits, and barefoot.

The sun beat down, but we were mostly in shade. A warm breeze blew and whistled between the rocks: WHEEE-HEEEEEE-WHEEE-EEEEE-WHEEE

"All we need now is a picnic lunch," Marco

said. "Tobias! Go rustle us up some juicy rats and toads."

<No need,> Tobias said coolly. <Just eat that snake you're sitting on.>

"Yaaahhh!" Marco screamed as he leaped to his feet and began slapping his behind frantically.

A small black snake slithered away from the pocket of warm sand where Marco had been sitting.

"I'm bit! I'm gonna die! A rattler bit my butt!"

<It's not a rattler, and he didn't bite you,> Tobias said. <He's just a harmless bull snake.>

"No snake is harmless," Marco muttered. "But keep your hawk eyes open in case a rattler does come for me."

<I will protect your butt from snake bite, Marco,> Tobias said solemnly.

"Let's just morph back," Rachel suggested. "We don't need to rest. I feel fine."

"There's no rush, is there?" I asked.

Morphing is tiring. It wears you out. Sometimes we've had to morph very quickly with no rest between shape changes. But that's not the best way to do it. You feel much more energized if you wait a little while.

Rachel shrugged. "No. No rush." She stretched up on her toes and looked around at the boulders. The WHEE-EEING wind caught her hair and blew it in her face. "It looks like some scene from an old Western. The good guys are up here in the rocks hiding from the bad guys. All we need is six-guns and rifles."

CHICK-CLICK!

<What the —> Tobias cried.

CHICK-CLICK! CHICK-CLICK!

I froze at the sound. I'd heard it before in real life. And I'd heard it on TV a thousand times. It was unmistakable. It was the sound of weapons being cocked.

I looked upward and there above us, pointed straight at our heads, were the black muzzles of automatic rifles.

I was so busy staring at the guns, it took a few seconds before I even noticed there were people holding the weapons. They wore helmets covered in camouflage fabric. Desert-style camouflage in shades of tan and beige. Their uniforms were desert camouflage, too.

Their faces were not friendly.

One of the soldiers stood up and put his hands on his hips. "Okay now, here's what we're going to do. The three of you are gonna lie down, facedown in the sand, and place your hands behind your heads, fingers laced together."

I thought, *The* three *of us?* Of course! They thought Tobias was a hawk.

"But we're not *doing* anything," Rachel protested, sounding pretty much like I remember her sounding years ago when her mom would catch us rifling through her closet looking for clothes to try on.

"You have illegally entered a restricted government facility," the man said. "And you are in a world of hurt. Sergeant! Search them for weapons or contraband. And someone chase away that big old hawk there. He's staring at me."

"Yes, sir, Lieutenant."

<You guys, just go along with them,> Tobias said as he opened his wings and began to fly off. <I'll keep an eye out for you. Just play dumb.>

"You heard him, Marco," Rachel whispered with an exaggerated wink. "Be yourself."

Naturally, Rachel was completely unafraid. But then, Rachel is never afraid. I was afraid. But that's because I'm sane, unlike Rachel.

The soldiers leaped down from the rocks and quickly searched us as we lay facedown in the sand. It was a quick search: We were wearing our morphing outfits.

"All right, get up. Put on your shoes," the lieutenant said.

I winced. Shoes! Oh, man, we'd never be able to explain this.

"No shoes, sir!" the sergeant said.

I saw the frown form on the lieutenant's face. "Hey. Wait a minute. It's a couple of miles back to the road. How'd you get here without shoes? For that matter, there hasn't been a car down that road all day. How did you get here at all?"

I looked at Rachel. Rachel looked at Marco. Marco put on a big grin and said, "It was the Martians, Lieutenant. We were dropped here by aliens."

CHAPTER 9

"My name is Captain Torrelli. I am in charge of security for this facility."

We were in a very small, very airless, very brightly lit room. There were no windows. And whenever the door opened you saw a guy in an Air Force uniform.

A tough-looking guy in an Air Force uniform.

A tough-looking guy in an Air Force uniform, cradling a small machine gun.

There was also a bulletin board. On it were small posters reminding everyone that "Security is our business." And exhorting everyone to tolerate "Zero Defects."

But there was also something more familiar that caught my eye. One of the little flyers was

for The Gardens. The Gardens is the big combination amusement park and zoo where my mom
is one of the vets. Below the flyer was a sign-up
sheet, bearing a lot of names.

"Hi, Captain," Marco said. "How's it going?"

The captain glanced over at the lieutenant
who had picked us up. The lieutenant just
shrugged.

"Now look, kids, maybe you don't realize it,
but you're in trouble," the captain said.

"Yes, sir, we realize we made a big mistake," I
said. "It was totally an accident. We didn't even
know there was anything back here in the Dry
Lands. And boy, we'd never, ever come back
again if you let us go, that's for sure."

I smiled innocently. I nudged Rachel and she
smiled innocently as well. I prayed that Marco
would get a clue and smile innocently so we
could just —

"So. Where do you keep the alien?" Marco
asked.

So much for Marco getting a clue.

The captain pressed his lips tightly together
until they turned pale. Then he said, "Look, kid,
this is an Air Force installation. We don't discuss
what we do here, but I am authorized to tell you
one thing: There are no aliens here!"

"Yeah, right. Sir," Marco snorted.

"What's your name, son?"

"Um . . . Mulder. Fox Mulder."

"Well, you are in a world of hurt, Fox Mulder. You have violated federal law. You could be thrown in prison!"

"Sir?" I interrupted. "Please just ignore Mar — I mean, Fox."

"Yeah. He's an idiot," Rachel added.

"He just likes to annoy people. We're just kids, you know. We didn't mean any harm. Couldn't you just give us a warning?"

"A very stern warning, even," Rachel agreed.

"Normally that's just what we'd do," the captain said. "We do get our share of Looney Tunes and crackpots out here." He looked directly at Marco as he said "crackpots." "However, we have ourselves a little mystery here. See, none of you is wearing shoes. The lieutenant's men searched the area — no shoes. And it is physically impossible to have walked across all that undergrowth and through those rocks without shoes."

"So we're busted for not having shoes?" Rachel asked.

"Look, what's the big deal, sir?" Marco asked. "If you have an alien here, why not just tell everyone?"

The captain gave Marco a long, hard stare. "I

57

want the three of you to write down your names and your parents' phone numbers on this piece of paper." He shoved a clipboard at Marco. "We're gonna call your folks. Maybe they'll appreciate your sense of humor."

I watched over Marco's shoulder as he wrote down "Fox Mulder." Then he followed it by a phone number.

Rachel identified herself as Dana Scully.

Then it was my turn. And I drew a total blank. See, I don't really watch *X-Files*. The captain stared at me as I held the pen poised over the paper and sweated.

What name? What name?

"Don't you know your own name?"

"Um . . . sure. It's . . . Cindy! That's it, Cindy. Cindy . . . Crawford."

Marco stared at me. Rachel stared at me. I wrote down the name with a trembling hand and then wrote in some random numbers.

The two officers left. There was a loud click from the lock closing.

"Cindy Crawford?" Marco demanded. "What are you, nuts?"

"Me? Me? How about you?"

"Every guy in the country knows who Cindy Crawford is!"

"We have to get out of here. Fast!" Rachel

said. "I gave him the phone number for Pizza Hut delivery."

"I gave him the number for the Sports Scoreboard recording," Marco said.

"I just gave him one-two-three-four-five-six-seven-eight!" I said.

"Eight? You gave him eight numbers?" Marco laughed. "Remind me not to ever be a spy with you. Now how do we get outta here?"

"I can morph to grizzly and —" Rachel started to say.

"No!" I cried. "These are good guys and, as far as we know, they're, not Yeerks! We can't hurt anyone! We need something small enough to get out beneath the door. I say housefly."

"I hate doing flies," Rachel shuddered.

"Ant?"

"No way."

"Cockroach?"

Rachel nodded. "Okay. I'll do cockroach."

Marco looked at her, mystified. "Flies gross you out but roaches don't?"

But Rachel and I were already busy morphing and Marco had to hurry to keep up.

This time the floor didn't rise toward us. It leaped! And the changes didn't involve the gentle, rather lovely transformation of skin into feathers.

This time the transformation started for Marco with antennae. Two huge, long, spiky antennae shot straight out of his forehead.

SPLEEET!

For Rachel the change began with the legs. The middle pair of legs. The ones that grew right out of her chest.

"Yah!" I yelled, even though I knew what to expect more or less. Still, seeing antennae come popping out of a friend's head and hairy, articulated legs from your best friend's chest . . . well, it is gross.

But I wasn't able to really focus too much on them. Because I was becoming distracted by the fact that one-foot squares of linoleum now looked as big as a front lawn. And by the fact that I could hear the sound of every bone in my body dissolving into mush. And by the fact that my skin was turning hard and smooth.

SPLOOOT! Legs popped out of my chest.

SPROUT! Antennae zoomed out of my head.

My own legs shriveled. I fell forward! I stuck out my hands to catch myself, but I no longer had hands.

"I've changed my mind," Rachel started to say jokingly. But whatever she had wanted to say next was lost because her pretty, human face turned hard and bronze, and her mouth split into the clicking mouthparts of a roach.

<What I was going to say was, "I've changed my mind, roaches *are* grosser than flies,"> Rachel said.

And that's when we felt vibrations through our antennae. The heavy vibrations of footsteps. Angry footsteps.

It took some practice to use roach senses well enough to understand speech. But we'd had practice. So we were able to hear the captain saying, "Pizza Hut, eh? I'll show the little monsters some Pizza Hut!"

<Move it, boys and girls!> Rachel cried with the giddy enthusiasm she always has when facing certain death.

<RAAAAID!> Marco yelled.

<Really funny, Marco. Really funny,> I muttered. <Can we just get the heck out of here?>

Air movement! Vibration! Wind! The scent of humans!

The door had been opened. It swept over our heads. We each motored our three pairs of legs. We were out of there!

CHAPTER 10

Zooooooooom!

We blew across highly polished linoleum squares.

My six legs motored insanely, my antennae waved wildly, my every cockroach instinct screamed, *Run! Run! Ruuuuun!*

So we ran.

Not that we exactly had any idea where to run.

<Where are we going?> Marco yelled.

<How would I know?> Rachel cried.

<Head for daylight!> I screamed.

<How do we tell daylight from plain old lights?>

<I don't know. Um . . . um . . .> I tried to

think of how a roach would know the difference between daylight and plain old interior lights. Of course! Roaches are startled and scared by lights. The brighter the light, the scarier it would be.

<Run toward whatever scares your roach brain worst!> I yelled.

<Oh, swell. This stupid bug brain is already scared to death.>

Vibrations! Lots of them. Big, heavy, earth-shaking. We're talking VIBRATIONS!

Through the muddy, fractured, nearsighted roach senses I saw, or at least felt, massive things falling from the sky. It was like someone was dropping trucks all around me!

Footsteps! Shoes as the same size as double-wide trailers!

WHOOOMPF! WHOOOMPF! WHOOOMPF!

<Look out! There's people walking on us!> Marco yelled.

WHOOOMPF! A monster killer shoe came down from the sky and slammed into the floor just an inch ahead of me. But the roach brain had reacted just in time. The roach brain knew how not to get stepped on.

<Let the roaches handle this!> I said. <The roach brains are good at this.>

WHOOMPF! My roach body scurried out of the way, barely avoiding the side of a heel that would have squashed me flat and dead in a split second.

<Daylight! I think I see daylight!> Rachel cried.

<Lead on!> I dimly perceived Rachel's roach morph ahead of me. And Marco was just beside me. All together, three scared-as-heck roaches blew toward a bright light.

Suddenly there was a ridge. Pretty high to me, even though it was probably not even an inch high. It was the transom of a doorway, I realized, and I knew one thing: I really wanted out of that building.

<Tobias!> I called out. <Can you hear me? Are you up there?>

<Yeah. Where are you?> he asked. <And *what* are you?>

<We are three lost little cockroaches in a big hurry!> Marco said.

<Got you!> Tobias said.

<Thank goodness for those hawk eyes,> Rachel said. <Now get us outta here!>

<Keep moving and try to bunch up together. And by the way, there's a column coming your way. A column of . . . vehicles.>

Something about the way he said "vehicles" should have alerted me. But all I could think about was getting close to Marco and Rachel so Tobias could pick us up.

We were on concrete now, and moving slower. When you're bug size, concrete doesn't look smooth. It looks like you're running across an endless field of small boulders. Concrete kind of glitters. At least that's how it looked to my cockroach senses.

And another thing about concrete, at least concrete with the sun beating down on it: It's hot!

<I'm gonna fry!> Marco wailed.

<Oh, man, it's hot! I didn't think bugs could feel temperature this much,> I said.

<Tobias! Hurry up, man, we're seriously getting barbecued!>

Suddenly a shadow swooped down. I had to fight the urge to panic and run in a completely different direction.

Huge, rough-textured talons came hurtling down at amazing speed. The nails scraped along the concrete. One talon hooked beneath me and lifted me up, up, up.

<Yeeee-hah!> Marco yelled. <Red-tailed airlines!>

No more heat. No more concrete. I was up in the air, wind whipping . . .

<Ahhhhhhhhhh!> I was falling! Tobias had lost his grip on me and I was falling, falling, spiraling, tumbling through the air.

How far I fell, I can't say. My cockroach

morph can't see farther than a few inches. But it seemed as if I was falling a long time.

Falling . . .

<Cassie!> Tobias yelled.

Falling . . .

<Cassie!> Rachel echoed.

<What about Cassie?> Marco asked.

<I dropped her!>

POOMPH!

I hit the ground. Dirt! It billowed up around me as I slammed into it.

But I was not hurt.

I was on my back. My legs pawed madly at the air. <How do you turn one of these things over?> I asked. I felt ominous thunder rumbling up through the ground.

<Cassie! I see you!> Tobias yelled. <I'm coming for you, but Cassie, you have to move! I can't make it in time! You have to move *now*!>

His tone was not exactly reassuring. <What's happening?>

<It's that column, Cassie. It's coming right at you!>

<Column? Of what, troops? Soldiers?>

<No. Tanks.>

And then I realized that wasn't thunder I was hearing and feeling.

CHAPTER 11

<Cassie! Move!> Tobias cried as he plummeted toward me in a full-speed stoop.

<I am moving!> I motored my roach legs like a roach caught in a sink. But I was pawing the air. And the thunder was more than thunder now, It was like a continuous, nonstop explosion.

BBBBRRRRRBBBRRRRRRMMMM! BBBBRRRRRBBBBBMMMMMM!

Wings! Wait! Roaches have wings. All I had to do was —

Too late!

<Cassie!>

Something blotted out the sun. I felt my little roach body pressed into the dirt. It seemed to last forever. The pressure was unbelievable! And yet . . .

Suddenly I was up off the ground. But not free. I was stuck. Stuck to the tread of a tank, and going slowly around as the tread came around toward the front of the tank again.

I scampered my legs again, but now two of them were not moving. I was stuck faceup on a dirty treadmill. I would not survive another crushing by the tank tread.

I tried my left wing. No good. It was squashed.

I tried my right wing. Yes!

I flipped over, landed on my four good feet, turned a sharp left and ran like a lunatic for the edge of the tread. ZOOOOM! I fell! I hit the dirt and I ran. I ran and ran and ran without even thinking about stopping.

Tobias lifted me up from the ground, and I was still running with my four good roach legs.

Marco seemed to think the entire thing was hysterically funny, of course. He laughed for the next ten straight minutes as Tobias flew us away from Zone 91. And while Marco laughed, Tobias apologized for dropping me.

Tobias set us down outside the boundaries of the secret base.

We demorphed in a gully formed by a small stream.

"Are you okay?" Rachel asked me, once she and Marco and I were all human again.

"Considering I was run over by a tank, yes, I'm okay."

Marco grinned. "I wish I could see the look on Captain Torrelli's face when he realizes we've all three disappeared."

Rachel punched Marco in the arm. "You moron! Why did you keep provoking him with all that alien talk? He would have let us go."

"Actually," Marco said, with no trace of his usual attitude, "he would *not* have let us go till he contacted our parents. And we couldn't have that, could we? So I deliberately provoked him because now he'll just write us off as another bunch of deluded wackos. If we'd seemed perfectly sensible he'd *really* wonder what we were doing there with no shoes."

Rachel glared at him suspiciously. But I knew Marco was right. Like I said, Marco's a clown sometimes, but he's not dumb.

"So now what?" Rachel asked. "It's getting late. We need to get home."

<You guys should morph as soon as you're ready. It'll be cooling down soon. Fewer thermals equals harder flying.>

I was starting to feel like an idiot. I was the one who seemed most concerned about the idea of Yeerks in horses. But we'd learned absolutely nothing. All we'd managed to do was get ourselves detained by the military police and almost squashed by a tank.

Rachel obviously was prepared to shrug off the horse-Controller idea. I think she halfway doubted we really did see that Yeerk crawl out of that horse.

The others were even more skeptical. And I could see their point: Our real problem was about Yeerks taking over humans. If they wanted to experiment with controlling horses, well, that was a pretty low priority.

<I hear something,> Tobias said. He was perched on a twisted, gnarled piece of dried up wood. <Everyone down. Hide till I see what it is!>

He flapped his wings and took off as Marco, Rachel, and I crawled down under a bush. Unfortunately, it was a thorny bush.

"Oh, *this* is fun," Marco muttered softly.

<It's just some horses. It's okay,> Tobias called down from the sky above.

Marco started to crawl out from hiding. I grabbed his arm. "No. Wait," I hissed.

A half dozen horses climbed stiffly down the side of the gully heading for the water. They were led by a gray stallion.

"See? Horses. Now can I get this thorn out of my butt?"

I shook my head and put my finger to my lips. I watched the horses climb down. I looked closely for anything that looked strange or unusual. But they sure looked like any old horses.

Four of the horses lowered their big heads and began to drink. A fifth horse stood guard.

The sixth horse was a very nice-looking roan that almost looked as if she'd come from thoroughbred stock. This mare paused beside the horse, standing guard and almost seemed to be whispering in his ear.

Then, suddenly . . .

PLOP! PLOPPLOPPLOP! PLOP!

The horse began to do what horses do. If you know what I mean.

"That horse is taking a dump," Marco whispered.

"Thanks for pointing that out, Beavis," Rachel said. "We wouldn't have noticed without you."

"Horse patties," Marco said. "Prairie pies. Heh-heh-heh-heh."

"That does it. I'm not sharing a bush with —" Rachel began to say.

"Shh! Look! Look!"

To my amazement, the horse who had been pooping stopped. The other horses looked over at her and neighed. I swear they were laughing.

And then the horse in question walked away, moved behind a tree out of sight of the other horses, and finished her business.

"A *modest* horse?" I asked smugly.

Rachel nodded. "Yeah. It does seem just a little weird."

We waited till the horses had finished drinking and moved on. Tobias flew down and landed beside us. I crawled out through the brambles and brushed myself off.

"I've never seen a horse hide behind a tree to do her business." I looked at Marco and Tobias. "Are you guys satisfied? These are *not* normal horses."

CHAPTER 12

The next day was Saturday. We met at my barn.

How do you spy on horse-Controllers? How do you observe the actions of a group of horses with Yeerks in their heads? That was the question.

"We morph horses, of course," I said as I pried open the jaw of the fox who'd been eyeing me hungrily when I was an osprey the day before. I popped a pill in his mouth, held it shut, and blew on his nose to make him swallow.

"Horses? Didn't you morph a horse once?" Jake asked me.

"Yes. I morphed one of our horses. It was amazing. But we have one problem: We only have the one horse here right now. She's got distinctive markings. And we can't exactly go walking around the Dry Lands looking identical."

"Identical horses," Marco mused. "Sweet Valley Horses. Hmmm. That could be a TV show."

We were all there together. All six of us, including Ax. Ax was in his human morph. Once again I was struck by just how weirdly handsome he was. It was strange how you could see little hints of Rachel, Marco, Jake, and me in him. There were some expressions, sometimes when he smiled, for instance, when it was like looking in a mirror and seeing a male *me*. It was a little creepy.

"Horses. Hore-hore-hore-sezuh," Ax said.

Marco spread his hands wide, palm up. "Is that it, Ax? Or was there more to your comments?"

"Horses are quadrupeds," Ax said. "Much more sensible than walking around perched on two rickety legs like humans do. Rickety. Rick-kuh-tee. Is that a funny word?"

"Yeah, 'rickety' is hysterical," Rachel said. "So, where do we find six different horses for us to morph?"

<The Gardens?> Tobias suggested.

I closed the fox's cage and wiped my hands on my jeans. "All they have at The Gardens are exotic horse breeds. We want horses who look like horses."

Mentioning The Gardens reminded me of the

sign-up sheet at the base. Should I mention it? No, it probably wasn't important.

"How about one of the farms around here?" Jake suggested.

I shook my head. "Everyone around here knows me. If they walked in on us . . ."

"The racetrack," Rachel said. "They have tons of horses out there. Usually a couple of dozen, at least. I've gone there with my dad. Last weekend, in fact. That's his idea of a cool place to take his daughters on visitation day."

"Did he let you bet?" Marco wondered.

"My dad placed it for me. Two dollars on Chase Me Charly to show. He came in second. I won three dollars."

I stared at my friend. You think you know everything about a person, then, suddenly, you find out something new.

"Humans bet? On horses? To see which is faster?" Ax asked. "What do you bet?"

"Money. What else?" Marco asked.

"Money. Ah, yes. Mon-nee. I always forget about humans and their money."

Jake looked at his watch. He was getting that slightly exasperated look he gets sometimes when no one is sticking to business. "Okay, look, we go to the track. No one bets. We acquire some horse DNA, then we fly out to the Dry Lands and spy on the modest horses."

"Again?" Marco moaned. "That's what we do *every* Saturday. When are we going to get to do something original?"

<Can I ask one question?> Tobias asked. <Why would the Yeerks be taking over the bodies of horses?>

"Good question," Jake said.

"It has to be about Zone Ninety-one," Marco said. "I mean, what is it, coincidence?"

"It may be about Zone Ninety-one, but not the way you think, Marco," I suggested. "Who knows what the Air Force is really doing out there? Maybe they're testing some new superweapon the Yeerks are afraid of."

Ax laughed. "A *human* weapon that would frighten the Yeerks? That isn't possible. Sible. Pah-si-bull."

I felt a little insulted on behalf of the human race. But Ax was probably right. "Look, I just don't see where the Yeerks would care about some kind of alien ship that may be hidden out there. It's nuts. Unless . . . unless maybe they don't know if the stupid conspiracy theory is true or not."

"I have to confess I don't really understand what you are all talking about," Ax said. "However, the Yeerks would know if there was something nonhuman anywhere on this planet's surface. Their sensors could do an analysis of the alloys. After all, the Yeerks are not exactly on the level of Andalites, but they aren't totally primitive. They would be able to detect the presence of alloys, plastic composites, or live metals — the sorts of things spaceships are built from."

I know Ax doesn't mean to sound condescending. But sometimes he ends up sounding that way just the same. Of course then he'll kind of spoil the whole Mr. Spock/Commander Data thing by saying something like:

"Is wood tasty? Is it good to eat?"

"Yeah, but you want to use plenty of salt," Marco replied.

Jake looked troubled. "You know, it would be really bizarre if the whole conspiracy thing turned out to be true. I mean, what if the government really has been hiding some alien spacecraft out at Zone Ninety-one?"

"What is a Zone Ninety-one?" Ax asked.

"For one thing, I'd have to apologize to Marco," Rachel said. "But for another thing, maybe whatever it is they have hidden out there at Zone Ninety-one really could be used to penetrate the secrets of Yeerk technology."

"Well, guess we better find out," Jake said. First stop: the racetrack."

"And what exactly is a racetrack?" Ax asked. "Zactly?"

CHAPTER 13

It wasn't far to the racetrack. We decided to fly. We all had seagull morphs except Ax and Tobias. We figured seagulls wouldn't be too obvious flying around the racetrack barns and paddocks. Whereas an entire sky full of birds of prey might be. So we all morphed seagulls, Ax did his harrier, and Tobias stayed Tobias.

Flying as a seagull is the same as flying as an osprey in most ways. But in some ways it can be very different: You have to flap a lot more; you fly closer to the ground; and seagull brains have a different way of looking at the world than bird-of-prey brains. Seagulls are scavengers.

We flapped up and away from the barn, working our sharp-edged, swept-back white-and-gray wings. Ax and Tobias soared far overhead, watching the sky for other predators.

But for the four of us seagulls, the trip was all one long garbage dump.

<Look! A Butterfinger wrapper! I think there's some left!>

<Look at that Burger King Dumpster! Oh, man, it's *loaded* with french fries and leftover burger!>

<Oh! Oh! Oh! Cheese puffs!>

<No way! Someone threw out a half-eaten chicken leg! Extra crispy!>

<Wouldn't that almost be cannibalism?>

<Didn't we have this discussion before?>

<Hey, it's extra crispy. I love extra crispy!>

Now, yes, we could have struggled harder to control the seagull's mental obsession for anything even approaching food. But it would have been hard. And to tell the truth, it was kind of fun. Seagulls can spot food you wouldn't even think of. You'd be amazed the stuff people just throw away.

<Look! Out behind that Pappa John's. Pepperoni!>

Anyway, we eventually made it to the racetrack. Without actually pausing to scarf any garbage.

From the air the track was a big, long, dirt oval outlined with a white rail fence. There was a high, covered grandstand on one side, and various long, narrow horse barns stretching out behind the stands.

The parking lot was about half full with cars and trucks pulling horse trailers. There was a good crowd of people, up in the seats and milling around beside the track itself.

Out in the middle of the oval track was a big electronic tote board. It was already posting the odds for the first race.

<Anyone see a good place to demorph?> Rachel asked.

<There must be some empty stalls in those barns,> Tobias suggested. <Just fly in and land.>

<Or we could go check out the trash behind the clubhouse,> Marco suggested.

<Seagulls,> Tobias sneered. <You might as well be pigeons.>

I guess to a hawk, calling someone a pigeon is a pretty bad insult.

We swooped low and fast along the back wall of a barn. The stalls were in two long rows, opening out to the outside on one side, and into a long connecting hallway on the other side. Sure enough, about half the stalls were empty.

I turned a sharp left. Seagulls can turn amazingly fast. And shot . . . ZOOOOM! . . . straight in through an open stall door.

I landed on the dirty hay. <Looks okay in here,> I called to the others.

ZOOOM! ZOOOM! ZOOOM! ZOOOM! ZOOOM!

The others flew in and landed near me. Then we began to demorph. It was easy. No problem.

Just one slight difficulty we'd overlooked: When you demorph you have to return to your normal body. For Rachel and Jake and Marco and me that meant human.

But for Ax that meant Andalite.

81

CHAPTER 14

<Okay, everyone, demorph,> Jake said. <Tobias? You want to go human or stay as you are?>

<I have to stay in hawk shape if I'm going to acquire a horse. In fact, while you guys demorph, I'll go ahead and try and find a horse I like.>

See, you have to be in your original form if you're going to acquire a new morph. And, sad as it may be, red-tailed hawk is now Tobias's true body. Tobias flew off, keeping his wings tight in the narrowness of the barn.

I began to demorph. My swept-back white wings grew fingers. My tiny legs sprouted up and up and up. My yellowish beak spread and softened to become lips.

And one thing was becoming clear: Four kids

and an Andalite are kind of crowded in a single stall.

Everyone was about ninety percent human, and Ax was about ninety percent Andalite, when suddenly, without warning, I found myself staring at two old, old men. One was chewing the end of a slobbery cigar. They were looking over the stall door.

"What the . . . what are you kids doing in that stall? And what in the name of all that's holy is *that*?"

What they were seeing was four kids who seemed to be wearing leotards decorated with feathers. And one really, really unusual creature like nothing either had ever seen before.

"Ax! Keep your head down!" I hissed. I leaped to get between the two old men and Ax's tail.

In case you've never seen an Andalite in person before, and obviously, you haven't, let me explain. Andalites look like a weird cross between a deer, a horse, a scorpion, and a human. They have the bodies of slender horses or large deer, except that their fur is blue and tan.

Their upper bodies seem almost human, until you get to the head, which is so totally *not* human you'd never mistake it. Like I said earlier, Andalites have no mouths. They eat by absorbing grass up through their hooves as they run. And they communicate telepathically with thought-speak. Plus, there's the whole eye thing.

Andalites have four eyes. Two are right where you'd expect them to be. The other two are at the end of flexible stalks atop their heads. You know the little hornlike things giraffes have? Picture those, only flexible. And with an eyeball at the end.

And finally, there's the tail. It's long and it ends in a scythe-shaped blade that could topple a tree faster-than-you-can-see.

The tail is what I was trying to hide from the old men. I could only hope that Ax would have the sense to keep his upper body lowered.

"I asked you kids what you're doing in that stall," the cigar man said, more sharply this time.

"Um . . . grooming our horse?" I offered.

Rachel's eyebrows shot up. "Our *horse*? Oh, yeah, that's exactly what we're doing. Grooming our horse." She reached over and stroked Ax's back.

"Small for a horse," the second man said skeptically. "What are you feeding that poor swaybacked nag?"

"Horse food," Marco said.

"Horse food?"

"Yeah. Um . . . you know, horse food. Boy, you should see how many cans this guy can eat.

Man, all day long I'm opening cans of horse food and filling his dish."

The two men stared. The cigar man moved his cigar to the other side of his mouth.

"Hah-hah-hah!" I practically screamed. "He's such a kidder! Of course we're not feeding our *horse food* from *cans*. We're feeding him alfalfa and hay. Like you'd feed any horse. My friend is such a joker! Total joke machine!"

"Plus he's a moron," Rachel added.

"Your horse is blue," the second man observed. "Never seen a blue horse."

"Never seen kids wearing feathers on their faces, either," cigar said. "And I've seen a lot of things in my time."

Jake was looking at me, waiting for me to come up with an answer. So was Rachel. So was Marco. Our "horse" was blue. There was no denying that. And yes, we had white-and-gray feathers sticking out of the sleeves and collars of our morphing suits.

"We like blue horses," I said lamely.

"Some day, all horses will be blue," Jake agreed.

"You kids step out of there. This ain't right. Not any part of this. Step out of there and let me see what —"

I felt, rather than saw, the twitch that ran through Ax's body.

"Ax, NO!" I yelled.

FWAPP! FWAPP!

He struck with his deadly tail! But not at the men. In less than a half-second he had sliced the overhead railing that framed the stall. He'd sliced right through it in two places. The railing, a chunk of eight-by-eight lumber, fell directly on the men's heads.

"Ahhh!"

"Owww!"

"Run!" Jake cried.

We stumbled and piled over the two groaning men. Four kids and a very strange blue "horse." Out of the corner of my eye I saw a flash of brown-and-russet feathers.

<I leave you guys alone for two minutes!> Tobias said. <And what have you done?>

"Get them! Stop those kids!"

We were off and running between the stalls! Ax was morphing to human as he ran. I was finishing my demorph, losing the last of the feathers. Outside the barn, crowds of people were milling around, waiting for the first race.

"Get out of here. Out into the grandstand!" Jake yelled. "We can lose ourselves in the crowd."

Then, WHAM! A stall door flew open, right in front of me. It cut me off from the others. I dodged around it, but too slowly. Someone grabbed my ankle. I sprawled, facedown on the concrete.

"Cassie!" Jake yelled. He started back for me, but now there were people pouring into the barn. Stable hands, jockeys, horse trainers, and owners, all worried about what we might have done to their horses.

I looked down. It was some teenager who had my ankle.

"I got one of them!" he yelled.

I didn't want to kick him. I didn't want to hurt him. He was just a guy, probably not a Controller.

"I got this one! I got this guy!"

Guy? Excuse me? *Guy?* I wasn't even wearing overalls or anything. Okay, maybe the workout suit I was wearing for morphing was less than stylish, but hey, *guy?*

Now I wanted to kick him.

WHAPP! I kicked his hand loose.

"Sorry," I said and scrambled to my feet. I looked around frantically. No Jake. No Rachel. No Ax or Marco or Tobias. All I saw was the back end of what looked like a small mob, chasing someone down at the far end of the barn.

I dodged behind the fallen teenager and threw myself into stall.

"Take it easy, boy," I whispered to the big golden stallion in the stall. "Take it easy. E-e-e-a-a-s-y."

Normally animals love me. This one didn't.

"HhhhREEE-hee-heee-heee!"

I had two choices. Get out of that stall and be captured. Or stay in the stall and be trampled. So I chose option number three.

See, when you acquire an animal's DNA, it seems to put them in a kind of trance. They remain very calm. Which is how it's possible to acquire a grizzly bear.

So I pressed both my hands against the heaving flank of the big horse and I focused my mind. He grew calm and quiet. His DNA flowed into me. It became a part of me.

"One of 'em is still in this barn somewhere," I heard a voice say.

Well. If you want to be inconspicuous in a horse barn, what are you going to do?

Exactly. I started to morph the horse.

CHAPTER 15

TA TA TA TA TATA TA TATA TA TA TA TAAAAH!

I heard the trumpet announcing the start of a race. And I heard the crowd outside in the grandstand murmuring in anticipation. But I had other things on my mind.

I had morphed a horse before. So I thought I knew exactly what to expect. But this was not just any horse. This was a racehorse. Highstrung, aggressive, and just a little mean.

"Search every stall!" a voice cried. "Who knows what those kids have been doing to the horses! They turned one horse blue!"

"Well, make it fast. The first race has already started."

I heard stall doors opening and closing. They were at the far end of the barn. I had two minutes. Maybe.

I started the morph.

The first thing that happened was the ears. My human ears sort of crawled up the side of my head to the top. Then they sprouted. No big deal. I mean, no big deal once you're used to that kind of thing. If you weren't expecting it and your ears suddenly started crawling up the side of your head while getting long and pointy and covered with golden fur, you'd probably think it was a pretty big thing.

My body began to change very quickly. My butt grew huge! I had megabutt! My knees suddenly reversed direction with a loud, sickening grinding noise. My calves were stretching out, longer and longer. They were practically without meat. Just long bones covered with golden fur.

The fur rippled up across my body. Up my legs. Down my arms. Across my back and chest. I wish I'd had time to enjoy that part because it was cool. The horse had a soft, smooth, beautiful golden coat.

Then my arms started growing. The upper arms bulged with massive, bunched muscles. All the muscle was at the top. The bottom was practically just a stick.

As I watched, my fingers melted together.

They looked exactly as if they'd been made of wax and put in a hot oven. They just melted.

"Ahh!" I yelped. For a brief moment I'd seen the fleshless bones of my own fingers. Not something you want to see. Trust me. They were bright white. I could see my fleshless knuckles.

"I heard something! Down there!"

"Just keep searching. No one is getting out of this barn."

I fell forward, no longer able to stand on my legs. I fell forward just as the bare bones of my fingers melted together and hardened into hooves.

CLUMP!

My front hooves hit the ground. And now the horse — the *real* horse — was starting to get extremely worried. He had come out of his "acquiring" funk. And now he was beginning to realize something very, very, *very* wrong was happening right there in his own stall.

"HreeEEE-heee-heee-he!"

"It's okay, boy," I started to whisper. But just as I started the word "okay," my entire face exploded outward.

My own nose just got up and left. It moved away. Far away. It sprouted into a muzzle a foot long. More than a foot long!

My nose grew so monstrously huge that it forced my eyes apart. It was incredible! My eyes, which had been just an inch apart, like any normal person's eyes, were spreading further and further. And as they separated, I found my field of vision growing wider and wider.

But then it was too wide! My eyes were staring out of the sides of my head. My eyes were where my temples should have been. And in between those eyes was a nose the size of Rhode Island. My nose had stretched out so far it had dragged my mouth along for the trip.

I heard an awful growling, grinding sound coming from inside my own head. My teeth itched as they were replaced by the thick, flat teeth of a horse.

I was now almost a complete horse. Then, somewhere way, way back, I felt a tail sprout like some hyperactive weed. Okay, now I was done.

The real horse stared at me from one big watery eye. It sniffed me. What it smelled . . . was nothing. At least to a horse brain. Horses and other animals that rely on smell are not equipped for the idea that they could smell another horse and have it smell exactly like them.

It would be like a human suddenly finding herself face-to-face with a person who was identical. Only horses aren't exactly the geniuses of the animal kingdom. They can't make any sense of it.

So, weirdly enough, the real horse's reaction

was to grow calmer. It was more or less as if I weren't there. And the stranger thing was that as I felt the horse brain in me awaken and bubble up beneath my own human consciousness, I felt the same way about the other horse.

It was like: What other horse?

I tested the horse's senses. Excellent hearing. Good sense of smell. But eyesight was a mess. I was nearsighted, but far worse than that was the way I was staring in opposite directions at the same time. My eyes looked left and right. I had no depth perception in those directions. I couldn't really tell very well if something on my left was two feet away or five feet. If you had put two sticks in the ground, I probably could not have told you which was closer.

But directly ahead of me, there was a zone where my horse eyes overlapped. Only there did I have binocular vision like humans and hawks have. I could see depth but only in the area right in front of me.

It was strange. But what was disturbing was the level of energy the big horse had. It was like every single muscle in my body was being given an electric jolt. I was an entire power plant of pure energy!

But there was nothing uncontrollable about the horse brain. I felt hunger, but not the raving, lunatic hunger of some species. I felt an edgy concern, but nothing like the insane, mind-eating fear of a small mouse or squirrel.

I can handle this, I told myself. *Just one thing left to do. I have to get out of the stall and out of the barn. And morph back and find the others. Okay, three things to do.*

There was just no way to be subtle about it. I stuck my big golden head out over the stall door and did what no horse has ever been smart enough to do: I slid the little lock to one side and pushed the stall door open.

Just act normal, I told myself. *Yeah. A normal girl who's turned into a racehorse.*

I stepped out. I could see in both directions simultaneously, so I saw the two groups of stable workers at opposite ends of the barn.

Ooookay. Just walk on down.

One of the men froze. He stared. And then he came rushing over. "Hey! It's Minneapolis Max! He's out of his stall. How the . . . someone is going to catch some grief behind this! Joe! Grab his bridle, for crying out loud! Quick, before Max here starts raising Cain!"

From the other side of my head I spotted the teenager I'd kicked earlier. He raced to the stall I'd just left. "Hey, Mr. Hinckley! There's another horse in here that looks exactly like —"

"Just shut up and bring me his gear! Now! NOW!"

"Yes, sir."

The man called Hinckley approached me slowly, carefully. With good reason. The horse in me was skittish. He was a combination of scared and mad. Mad at the man, sure. But much madder at the smell of the other stallions in other stalls. One in particular. His scent stuck in my nostrils and really, really annoyed me.

I didn't know what that other stallion thought he was doing on *my* turf, but I was ready to go hoof-to-hoof with him and show him who was boss!

"HrrrEEEE-hee-hee-hee HRRRR-EEEEE-heee-heee-he!" I whinnied at ear-splitting volume, screaming my challenge to combat.

"Hey, boy. You know you're in the next race so you decided to come on out? Save that energy, big guy. That's my champion! That's my Minneapolis Max."

That's when it hit me. I'm no racing fan. But the name penetrated my slightly deranged consciousness. I recognized that name.

I had just morphed the horse who was expected to go on to win the Kentucky Derby.

"Come on, boy, we have a race to run."

That was fine with me. I wanted to run.

CHAPTER 16

<Cassie. It's me, Tobias. I don't know if you can hear me, but you're the only one I haven't found. If you can, give me some kind of sign, anything. Where are you?>

<I'm down on the track,> I said.

<Hey! You must be in morph if you're thought-speaking!>

<Yes, I am definitely in morph.>

<Well, where are you? *What* are you?>

<I'm in horse morph, Tobias.>

<Cool. So where are you?>

I sighed. <Look at the track. See the horses being led into the starting gates? See the horse whose jockey is wearing red-and-green silks? Number twenty-four?>

<You're kidding.>

<No, Tobias. I am not kidding.>

<How did this happen?>

<It's a long story. And I don't have time to tell it. I have a race to run.>

My jockey was barely a feather on my back. That didn't bother me. But I really did not like the bit in my mouth. It was infuriating! Almost as infuriating as the dark brown stallion one stall over.

I snorted defiantly at the brown stallion.

"Easy. Easy," the jockey said.

Out of my right eye I spotted Marco pushing his way through the crowd. He waved frantically.

<I see you, Marco. It's okay, don't worry.>

Obviously, Tobias had told the others of my predicament.

"Who's worried?" Marco yelled. "I just want to know if you're going to win. I have five bucks I could bet on you!"

<Very funny. Oh, very, very funny.>

My jockey yanked my bridle and dug his toe into my side. And the dumb thing was, I didn't really know what he wanted me to do. See, I had the instincts of the horse I had morphed. But I did not have the lifetime training of the professional racehorse named Minneapolis Max.

So I had to actually think about it. With my human brain. I was pretty sure he wanted me to move toward the starting gates. So I did.

A trainer was standing by the gate. Cigar-man. The cigar was even more disintegrated by slobber now.

"He's always balky at the gate," Cigar-man said to the jockey.

Oh, really? Well, I would show them. I tossed my head proudly and I walked calmly into the narrow gate.

But once inside, I realized why Minneapolis Max was balky. There was zero room. The wooden slat walls pressed in on me from both sides. It was a trap! A trap!

Run!

I reared up, flailing my front legs wildly. I kicked the gate with my forehooves and yelled at the top of my horse lungs.

WHAM!

"HreEEE-heee-he!"

"Take it easy, Max, easy," the jockey said.

I was scared. Or at least my horse brain was scared. And I still had the obnoxious scent of that other big stallion in my nose. So I was mad, too.

That's my excuse. I just wasn't thinking. Because when the jockey once again told me to take it easy, I did something I shouldn't have done. Something I wouldn't have done if I hadn't been distracted.

<*You* take it easy. I'm crammed into a little box here!> I said in thought-speak.

Thought-speak is like E-mail: It only goes to the person you address it to. So he did hear me. I know for a fact he did because he said, "Huh? Wah? What the?"

BRRRRIIINNNNNG!

WHAP!

A massively loud bell rang, the gate slammed open, and I started running.

I kicked out with the big, bunched muscles of my back legs. I threw my front legs out to catch myself with each stride. I exploded from the gate. Exploded!

I felt the adrenaline flood my system. To my left, horses! To my right, horses! We were running all out. Running like mad, hooves flashing, muscles firing and releasing, manes streaming, tails bobbing, our nostrils flared wide to suck in gasping breaths.

I ran. I ran, and the other horses faded from my thoughts. I ran, and it was like I was the only horse on Earth. I saw the track ahead of me, and that's all I cared about. I just wanted to run and run for as long as there was open ground ahead of me.

I was doing what I had been designed to do. I was fulfilling millions of years of horse evolution.

I was running. And running was what I did. Running was what I *was*.

The jockey tried to rein me in. He was conserving my strength and stamina for the end of the race.

<Forget winning,> I told him. <The point is not to win. The point is just to run.>

To his credit, he didn't fall off in shock. And also to his credit, he gave me control, and I did what horses do:I hauled hoof.

Around the turn, digging my hooves in to keep from slipping. I moved in toward the white-washed rail, cutting straight across the path of another horse. But I didn't care. Hah! I was running! Everyone else could just get out of the way!

Down the backstretch. No sound but my own gasping breath and the pounding, pounding, pounding of dozens of hooves on dirt.

The far turn! I was tiring now. My lungs ached. My muscles burned. I felt each new impact of my hooves on the dirt. It was time to slow down. Rest a little.

But then I saw him. The dark brown stallion. I saw him sneak up, getting between me and the rail. And I saw him pull ahead of me.

"Don't fade on me now, talking horse!" the jockey said.

I saw the wild, triumphant look in the stallion's eye. It made my blood boil.

<Hang on, Mr. Jockey. We're gonna win this race!>

Easier said than done. The other horse was fast. Very fast. But I had something he didn't have: a human brain. See, I knew the finish line was not far off. I knew that I could pour every last ounce of energy into running. I could override my horse instincts that told me to slow down.

I stretched out my stride and powered down the track.

I was ahead!

He was ahead!

I was ahead!

He was ahead!

The crowd was screaming deliriously. I saw thousands of faces flash by, all with their mouths wide open. The roar just gave me more energy still.

The finish line!

FLASH! FLASH! The cameras went off.

ZOOM! I blew across the line. Exactly two feet ahead of the other stallion.

I had won!

I think it was the first time in my entire life I'd ever won any kind of athletic contest. Sure, I was a horse, but hey, a victory is a victory.

CHAPTER 17

Fortunately, in between running from stable hands and trying to find me, everyone in the group had managed to acquire a horse morph.

We flew out to the Dry Lands. It was a long trip, made even longer by the fact that the entire time we had the same conversation, over and over.

<All I'm saying is think of how cool it would be,> Marco pleaded. <We morph racehorses —>

<I don't think so, Marco,> Jake said.

<— then, using our human abilities we figure out if we think we can win, and the others put money down.>

<Not happening, Marco,> Rachel said.

<We start out betting whatever we have saved. Like I have about twenty dollars. But if we bet that at say, three-to-one odds, before you know it —>

<Marco, forget it, okay?> I said. <It wouldn't be right.>

<— we'd have sixty dollars. Bet that at three-to-one odds you have a hundred and eighty. Then bet that and you have five forty! Then sixteen hundred twenty! Then four thousand eight hundred and sixty!>

<How is it you can multiply in your head like that?> Rachel asked. <You barely scrape by in your math classes.>

<It's a whole different thing when you're multiplying money,> Marco said. <A whole different thing.>

We repeated this conversation with small variations all the way to the Dry Lands.

<Hey,> Tobias said. <I think we're in luck. Isn't that the same bunch of horses we saw before?>

<The modest horses?> Jake asked.

<Yep. That is them,> Tobias confirmed. <I remember the markings. Look at the way they move.>

Down below, my osprey eyes spied the horses. They were walking almost in a line. Like soldiers.

Not like wild horses. But alongside the disciplined group were other horses. These other horses were moving normally.

<I think our main group of horse-Controllers has picked up a few tagalongs. It would make sense. The real horses don't know these are Yeerk-infested horses. So they hook up, figuring to be part of the same herd.>

<And look where they're heading,> Marco said. <Right toward the base. Right into Zone Ninety-one.>

<I understand what a racetrack is now: a place where horses chase each other in circles as humans scream. But what exactly is this Zone Ninety-one?> Ax asked. <You were all talking about it before, but I am still confused.>

<*You* probably already know what's going on at Zone Ninety-one,> Marco said darkly.

Jake sighed. <It's a secret base. They say it's a place where the government is hiding an alien spacecraft that supposedly crashed here about fifty years ago.>

<Who is *they?*> Ax asked.

<Marco is *they,*> Rachel said. <Nuts. Wackos. Conspiracy freaks. People who go on the Internet and call themselves DarkTruth or whatever.>

<Ah,> Ax said, like he understood.

Marco was right about one thing, however: The horses were heading directly into the base.

Of course, so were other horses. Horses not connected to the band of horse-Controllers.

<If you want to infiltrate a heavily guarded base, what better way?> I admitted. <I saw horses wandering through the base when we were there.>

<True,> Jake said. <And if you want to watch a group of horse-Controllers, what better way than to join the herd, just like those others did? Let's fly up ahead. Morph to horse. And join up with this bunch. See where they go. What they do.>

<Power those wings,> Tobias said cheerfully. <We still have some flying to do.>

<All I'm saying is, think of how cool it would be,> Marco began again.

It took ten minutes to get far enough ahead of the horse-Controller herd with its stray tagalongs. We hid behind some rocks and morphed into our horse bodies. This time we did it quickly. Before base security could begin to think someone was in the rocks.

Once we were morphed I realized we had a problem. <We look way too good to be scruffy old wild horses,> I said. <We need to roll in the dirt a little. Run through some brambles. Look like we've been living out in the wild, not in pampered barns.>

By the time the horse-Controllers passed by,

we were six dirty, dusty, scruffy-looking beasts. But we were also the coolest-looking wild horses anyone would ever see. After all, one of us could be going on to win the Kentucky Derby.

<Here they come,> Jake said. <Just try to act natural.>

The horse herd came ambling by. A couple of the "real" horses raised their heads to give us a suspicious look and a sniff. But the horse-Controllers totally ignored us.

I resisted my idiot horse urge to challenge the other stallions to mortal combat. We fell into step, not close, but not too far from the others.

And we walked, with the slow CLOP-CLOP-CLOP of horses, right into the heart of the fabled Zone 91.

CHAPTER 18

The whole herd of us wandered onto the base. We wandered past even more intense warning signs. The last one actually said YOU MAY BE SHOT. We wandered right past men and women armed with submachine guns.

No one suspected horses.

Of course, if anyone had heard what we heard next, they would definitely have been suspicious.

"Hullak fimul fallanta gehel. Callis feellos."

<Who said that?> I asked.

<Um . . . that horse said it,> Rachel said.

"Yall hellem. Fimul chall killim fullat!"

<And that was another horse. We're trapped in a *Mister Ed* rerun,> Marco said. <We are in the *Nick at Night* zone.>

<That's *Galard!*> Ax said. <They're speaking *Galard!*>

<Two questions,> Jake said tersely. <What's *Galard,* and can they hear us thought-speak? And answer the second question first.>

<No. They can't hear us. *Galard* is a sort of universal language spoken by different races throughout the galaxy. It's what people speak when they come from different species and don't share the same language. These horses must have been fitted with speech synthesizers.>

<Why wouldn't Yeerks be speaking Yeerk or whatever?> I asked.

<I don't know,> Ax admitted. <But the standard speech synthesizers use *Galard*. Maybe they acquired less sophisticated speech synthesizers. Sometimes it's easier to get older, less cutting-edge technology.>

<You mean they bought speech synthesizers on sale?> Rachel asked.

<At the Pluto Wal-Mart,> Marco said.

<Ax, can you understand what they said?> Jake asked.

<Yes, of course. They said to follow the plan. "If we do this right we'll be off this idiotic assignment, out of these idiotic stupid bodies, and back onboard ship where we belong." That's what the leader said.>

<Uh-oh,> Tobias said darkly. <They're split-ting up.>

<We'll have to split up, too. Follow each group,> Jake advised. <Me, Cassie, and Tobias go with one group, Ax, Rachel, and Marco go with the other. Ax? Listen to them if they talk any-more. And let us know by thought-speak.>

<Yes, Prince Jake.>

<Have I mentioned don't call me prince?>

<Yes, Prince Jake, you have.>

I fell in step alongside Jake, trying to look like any old horse walking along, minding her own business.

<This is weird,> I said. <These horses are def-initely on a mission. I'm almost surprised no one has ever noticed how bizarre their behavior is.>

<What sane person would ever even think that a horse would be a security risk?> Tobias said.

<How do you like horse morph, Tobias?> I asked, making conversation to ease my nervous-ness.

<Compared to flying? It's dull. Compared to the old days when I wouldn't have been able to morph with you guys at all? It's great!>

We were at the side of a road. This part of the base was densely built up with low, whitewashed clapboard buildings, each bearing stenciled numbers. Not far away was a large building with a half-filled parking lot. I couldn't see well enough with my dim horse eyes to read the sign above its door, but people were coming out, pushing loaded grocery carts.

<Base Exchange,> Jake explained. <Kind of a shopping center for the people stationed here.>

<Must be boring out here,> Rachel said. <Not much to do but keep secrets.>

A pair of Humvees loaded with uniformed troops came racing down the road. We stepped back out of the way. Totally unhorselike behavior. No one noticed. The guys in the Humvee never even glanced our way. They'd seen wild horses hundreds of times.

The afternoon sun was intense. It was really hot. The horse part of me wanted to go find a nice shady patch and rest. I saw some trees and picnic tables off to one side of the Base Exchange. People were carrying slices of pizza and baskets of fried chicken and potatoes out to the tables.

It was so weird. I was a human in a horse morph. I was walking along with Yeerks inside horse bodies. And we were, all of us, trying to figure out what, if anything, was being kept secret on this base.

Was it true? Had a spaceship crashed here back in the fifties? Had the government hidden it all these years? Were the Yeerks determined to get it away from the humans in order to keep us from understanding its technology?

What could be hidden on this base? A Yeerk Bug fighter? An Andalite fighter? Some ship belonging to some other race?

<Hey, Jake? Tobias? Do you smell anything weird?> I asked.

<I smell those french fries over at the Base Exchange,> Jake said.

<No, not that. Smell the horse-Controllers.>

<Do I have to? Hey . . . wait . . . you mean *that* smell?>

<Fear,> Tobias said. <Nervousness. Great. If they're scared, we should be scared.>

<I have that covered,> I said dryly.

I looked around, trying to make sense of the emotions I was literally smelling. I saw the second group of horse-Controllers. I saw Rachel, and Marco, and Ax along with a couple of tagalong horses. They were converging with us. Converging on the same building.

It was one of the hangars. A very large hangar, maybe fifteen stories high, with doors you could walk a dinosaur through. And it was a very secure hangar. There were guards at the main doors. Guards at every corner of the building. Looking up, I thought I saw the outline of a man with a rifle up on top of the structure.

There was a sign on the side of the building. I squinted but could not read it with my dim horse eyes.

<I miss my *real* eyes,> Tobias grumbled.

BRRRRRIINNNNGGGG! BRRRRRRIIIINNN-NNGGGG!

An insanely loud bell went off. I reared up before I could control the reaction. But the horse-Controllers showed no response at all. No response except to grow very still and very focused. They were expecting the bell.

The bell was a safety alarm. It was heralding the opening of the main doors of the hangar. I saw the guards move their automatic weapons down off their shoulders and into easy firing position.

KRRR-Chunk! Rrrrreeeeeeeeeee!

The doors began to open, motors whining loudly in my horse ears.

And that's when the second group of horses started to run. Three horse-Controllers, followed, after a moment's hesitation, by Marco, Ax, and Rachel, suddenly broke into full-out gallop straight for the hangar door.

<Oh, man,> Tobias groaned. <Why do I get the feeling there's going to be shooting soon?>

<Why are they doing that?> I asked. <It makes no sense. Why hide in horse bodies so you

can come and go without anyone noticing, and then suddenly do this?>

<Because the subtle approach isn't working,> Jake said grimly. <Remember what they said earlier: Do this and they're out of here. It's a final desperation move.>

<So what do we do?>

<We play follow-the-leader,> Jake said grimly. <And we hope these Yeerks have a good plan.>

Suddenly, our group of horse-Controllers surged forward. I was startled, but I quickly ran after them, followed by Jake and Tobias.

The first group was racing full tilt toward the hangar. They were almost there. The armed guards were watching them in bemusement. But you could see the bemusement turning to puzzlement. And finally . . . too late . . . fear.

WHAM!

The lead horse slammed bodily into one guard, knocking him into a second guard. Hooves flashed as the horse ran over the guard. I could see it, even with my weak horse eyes, because we were close now. Running straight for the door of the hangar.

We were there!

A madhouse! Guards mingling with seemingly insane horses. Guards being knocked to the ground.

"Get these horses outta here!" someone bawled.

"Neigh-heh-heh-heh!" the horses screamed.

"Sarge, what do we do?"

"Ahhhh!"

"HrrrEEEE-heee-he-he!"

"Shoot 'em!"

"Negative, soldier, do not fire! We could hit what's inside!"

Our group jumped into the melee of frantic soldiers and madly dancing, rearing, screaming horses. But our group stayed close together and plowed straight through.

Straight through and into the Most Secret Place On Earth.

CHAPTER 19

Into the hangar we thundered!

My hooves scrabbled on smooth, painted concrete. Through the eyes on the side of my head, I saw flashes of heavy equipment, banks of computer consoles, and flashing numerical readouts.

There were men and women in white lab coats running as if we were a pack of wolves or something. There were uniformed airmen running after us, waving their guns in the air. There were stuffy old officers with medals on their chests, standing with hands on hips and outraged expressions on their faces.

And everyone was yelling.

"What the blazing Hades is going on here?"

"Stop those horses!"

"Shoot!"

"Don't shoot!"

"Help! I'm allergic to horses!"

It was nuts. But the truth is, in a weird way, it was fun, too. Minneapolis Max was running. And when he was running, he felt fine.

Every nerve in my big horse body was tingling. I was incredibly alive with fear and excitement and the lust for competition. I wasn't some plow horse! I was a running fool. I was a born and bred champion! A big, tough, dominant stallion!

Yee hah!

"HREEE-HEEE-He-he!" I screamed for no reason, scaring a woman in a lab coat into dropping her open yogurt on the floor.

We thundered by, our weird herd of real horses, Yeerk-infested horses, and Animorphs in horse morphs.

And then we came to the room. You could tell it was the center, the nexus, the reason for all the security.

<It's gonna work,> Marco exulted. <We're in! We're in!>

It was glass on all sides. Glass that looked like it could be a foot thick. Through that glass we saw a pedestal of shining steel. And all around that pedestal were cameras, sensors, wires, lights, glowing screens, and rows of massive computers.

Bathed in the light, high on the pedestal, was something not from this planet.

It was about eight feet across. The shape was like a cube with the corners rounded off. The entire surface was covered with tubing and painted symbols.

At one end was an opening, large enough for a person to walk inside. I could just barely get a glimpse of the inside. It was smooth, a lovely green in color, with soft lighting. There was some sort of instrumentation on one wall.

<That's it! That's it! The most closely guarded secret in all of history!>

I've never heard Marco sound happier.

Jake and Ax and Marco and I, along with three or four horse-Controllers, all stared transfixed at what Marco had called "the most closely guarded secret in all of history."

"*Cullem fallat?*" one of the horse-Controllers asked.

<He wants to know what it is,> Ax translated.

"*Jahalan fornella,*" another horse-Controller said.

I didn't even need Ax's translation to understand: The Yeerks had no idea what it was.

They had succeeded. They had busted in.

117

They had laid eyes on the big secret. But they had no clue as to what it was.

"SERGEANT! GET those HORSES out of my facility! NOW!" a colonel bellowed.

"Yes, sir!" the sergeant yelled. "Horses! About face!"

It must have surprised the poor sergeant when, amazingly, we all complied. Animorphs and Yeerks, we turned and walked away.

CHAPTER 20

It was getting dark by the time we walked away, none the wiser, from the Most Secret Place On Earth.

The horse-Controllers walked glumly away into the Dry Lands. We shadowed them, keeping just a little distance. We'd been in morph for more than an hour. But Jake decided we should stay a while longer.

<I don't get this,> Marco complained. <I don't get this at all. It was a success! The Yeerks did it. They broke into the hangar. They saw . . . we all saw what was in there. So why are they depressed?>

<Ax says they don't know what it is they saw,> Jake pointed out.

<It didn't look like a spaceship,> Rachel said. <But it was definitely something alien.>

<Yeah, but what?> I said. <If the Yeerks don't know, and we don't know, and probably the scientists back at the base don't know, then what's the point?>

<"It is a tale told by an idiot, full of sound and fury, signifying nothing." Shakespeare,> Tobias said. <Every conspiracy nut in the world is obsessed by what's back there in that hangar. We saw it, and we don't even know what it is.>

<Actually . . .> Ax began. Then he stopped.

<Actually, *what?*> Rachel pressed.

<Oh, well . . . I sort of know what it is. It's kind of —>

<Look!> I yelled. Something was swooping in fast across the darkening desert. It flew along the ground, just inches above the scattered scruffy trees. It churned up the dust as it came. It was smallish, no bigger than a large human fighter plane. But it was shaped like a streamlined, headless beetle. There were long, serrated points aimed straight forward on either side.

<Bug fighter!>

I had to resist the urge to run. That was only natural. But what was strange was that once more I smelled fear from the horse-Controllers. They were scared of that Bug fighter. More scared than they'd been in rushing the hangar.

120

Or, more likely, scared of who was *in* that Bug fighter.

The Bug fighter swooped overhead, circled, and came to land in a pile of rocks.

<I can't believe the radar back at the base doesn't pick that up,> Tobias said.

<Radar. Is that the human tool that bounces radio beams off objects? I don't mean to offend, but any Andalite child could build a radar-cloak from the pieces of his toys.>

<Somehow you are grinding my nerves, Ax,> Rachel said grumpily. <And that's supposed to be Marco's job.>

We followed the horse-Controllers around the back of the rocks. The Bug fighter was waiting there, already on the ground. But the door didn't open until the horse-Controllers were assembled before it. Fear was radiating from them.

So much fear. It gave me a pretty good idea who was in that Bug fighter.

The door of the Bug fighter opened.

Out stepped a Hork-Bajir warrior. Seven feet of razor-bladed death. The Hork-Bajir swung his horned snakehead left and right, all the while holding a portable Dracon beam weapon.

Then, when it looked safe, the other occupant of the Bug fighter stepped out into the rapidly cooling air.

He was an Andalite. At least, he had an An-

dalite body. But of course he was no true Andalite.

<Visser Three,> I said. It was not a surprise.

<Yeah,> Jake said grimly. <Suddenly all this
just got more serious.>

Visser Three: leader of the Yeerk forces on
Earth. Leader of the invasion. The only Yeerk in
all of history to successfully seize control of an
Andalite body. The only Yeerk in all history to
gain the Andalite morphing power and Andalite
thought-speak abilities.

Our greatest enemy. The human race's greatest enemy.

<Report,> he said in a tone of complete casu-
alness.

The lead horse-Controller began to reply in
Galard. "Visser, *gahallum fillak —*"

<Don't waste my time. Did you succeed? Or
did you fail?>

"Visser, *kir fillan —*"

FWAPPPP!

The visser's Andalite tail moved so swiftly it
cracked the air. The deadly blade stopped a mil-
limeter from the horse-Controller's throat. A
twitch would send his head rolling.

<Did you penetrate the facility, yes or no?>

According to Ax, the horse-Controller answered yes.

<Did you see the object the humans are hid-

ing in there? The object we know is constructed of nonhuman alloys?>

Again, he answered yes.

<And can you now tell me what it is?>

The horse-Controller hesitated. And that's when the visser twitched his Andalite tail.

<Fools! Idiots! Incompetents!> the visser screamed in enraged thought-speak. <Weeks have been wasted setting up this effort. First we lose that clumsy fool, Korin Five-Four-Seven, when he was bitten by a snake. And now we've lost poor Jillay Nine-Two-Six!>

The visser indicated the no-longer-in-one-piece horse-Controller, like it had been someone else's fault he'd been lost.

<And now you don't even know what you saw?>

He was enraged. And Visser Three mad is beyond dangerous. His horse-Controllers backed away as far as they dared.

<I will have the secret!> the visser said in a suddenly low, sinister, thought-speak voice. <I will have it!>

For a while no one moved or spoke or even breathed. No one, me included, wanted to take any chance of attracting the furious visser's attention.

Then, <All right, I've punished the one responsible. Transport will come for the rest of you.

We still have the backup plan. It was always the better plan. We'll simply take control of a few of the humans working at this base. Have you idiots at least identified the right targets to infest?>

"*Jihal*, Visser!" one of the horse-Controllers said.

<Good. Then you can live. We'll target the right humans, and seize them tomorrow at . . .> Suddenly he stopped. <Those horses. What are they doing with you? They are not our people.>

In *Galard*, the horse-Controller explained that it was normal for horses to herd together. It was good for real horses to be there. It provided camouflage of sorts.

This was not the answer the visser wanted to hear. He aimed his Andalite stalk eyes directly at me. <Fool, do you not realize that the Andalite bandits who plague us can morph any animal they like, including horses? I will have to kill these creatures, just to be sure.>

<No one move. No one act like they heard anything,> I hissed to the others. I lowered my big golden head and crunched up a mouthful of grass. And then I did what horses do. And I wasn't modest about it.

The visser laughed derisively. <I suppose they are real horses, after all.>

I took a relieved breath.

<Still, better kill them.>

<Uh-oh,> I said.

The Hork-Bajir warrior leveled his Dracon beam at us. A second Hork-Bajir came running from inside the Bug fighter.

I felt a thrill of terror. I ordered myself to run away. But I wasn't the only creature in my head right then. Minneapolis Max was in there, too. And he didn't feel like running away.

My hindquarters bunched up and fired every muscle fiber at once. And, before I knew what was happening, I was running. But not running away. I ran straight for the first Hork-Bajir.

"HrrrEEEEE-HEEE-he-he!" I whinnied. I reared up, all the way back till I was standing on my hind legs, and I flailed madly with my forehooves.

I couldn't exactly aim my hooves, mind you. Horses aren't predators. But I flailed away and just as the Hork-Bajir was pressing the trigger . . .

BONK!

"Raaahhhh!" the Hork-Bajir bellowed. He dropped the Dracon beam from his hands. It clattered on the ground, and down I came. I landed directly with both hooves on the weapon.

CRUNCH!

I'd like to say it was deliberate. But the truth is that with my side-vision horse eyes I could barely even see my hooves, let alone aim them. But sometimes luck is as good as skill.

125

<Haul butt!> Jake yelled.

Now Minneapolis Max was ready to run away. So I ran. We all ran.

The two Hork-Bajir took off in pursuit.

<If they catch us, we're dog food,> Rachel said. <Two Hork-Bajir versus six horses? Not a prayer.>

She was right. And to be honest, if it had been a hundred horses versus two Hork-Bajir, the horses would have lost. <How fast are Hork-Bajir?> I asked Rachel. She had morphed a Hork-Bajir once.

<Fast,> she said grimly.

We bolted. We hauled. But the two bounding Hork-Bajir were hot on our trail.

Then we saw spotlights bouncing wildly toward us. Humvees! The security troops from the base were coming out to investigate.

We ran and the Hork-Bajir hesitated. When I looked back next, they were gone.

<Well, that was stupid from start to finish,> Rachel said as we got far from Zone 91. <We could have gotten killed. And for what? Over something even the Yeerks don't recognize.>

<Whatever that thing is, it sure doesn't look like a spaceship,> Marco admitted.

<Or a secret weapon,> Jake said. <And it doesn't look human, but who knows?>

<It is not a spaceship,> Ax said. <Or a weapon. But it is also *not* human.>

<Well, I guess we'll probably never find out what it is,> I said with a sigh.

<Why won't you find out?> Ax asked.

<Because it's not worth risking our lives again,> I said. <If the Yeerks don't even know what it is —>

<Of course the Yeerks don't know what it is,> Ax said calmly. <They have never been aboard an Andalite Dome ship.>

One by one, we each stopped walking. One by one we turned to face Ax.

<Ax, are you telling us you do know what that thing is?> Tobias asked.

<Of course. I started to tell you, but we were interrupted.>

<So? So what is it?> Marco demanded.

<It's a disposable module of a type used in the old days on the first generation of Andalite Dome ships. When the modules were used up, they were jettisoned into space. They were supposed to be aimed toward a star, so they'd be burned up without a trace. This one must have drifted through space, eventually being caught by Earth's gravity.>

<So it's a space engine?>

<It's a weapon?>

127

<No, of course not. It's . . . well, this is a bit embarrassing. It's an Andalite Dome ship's modular waste disposal system.>

For about a full minute, no one said anything. Then Marco spoke. <You're telling me the Most Secret Place On Earth, the fabled Zone Ninety-one, the Holy Grail of conspiracy nuts, is hiding the secret of an Andalite *toilet?*>

<Only a very primitive model,> Ax said condescendingly. <Since those days there have been huge technological improvements.>

CHAPTER 21

We got out of horse morph and into bird morph and flew home.

We alone now knew the secret of Zone 91. An entire base built to analyze what they thought was an alien spaceship but was, in reallty, a high-tech Andalite Porta-John

There was, according to Ax, absolutely zero chance that the Andalite toilet would give humans the ability to fly through space.

We had done some very important things as Animorphs. We had fought some terrible and vital battles.

This wasn't one of them.

I got home just in time to walk into my living

room and realize both my parents were waiting for me.

They had their angry-parent faces on.

"Where have you been?" my mother demanded.

Mom always takes the lead in discipline. She knows my dad will give in too easily. She thinks she's tougher. She thinks that because it happens to be true.

"I was out with Rachel," I said, more or less truthfully.

"Out with Rachel doing what?" my mom hissed. "You missed dinner. It's dark out. You didn't tell us where you were going."

My mom isn't a real big person. Until she's mad. Then she somehow gets larger. She seems to rise up and tower over me. It's weird. I mean, normally she's maybe two inches taller than me, but right then she was at least eight feet tall.

"We were very worried," my father said in a soft, quiet voice.

I sighed. I could feel the guilt welling up inside me. I hate it when they say they've been worried. See, I understand about worry now. I feel worry all the time for Rachel and Jake and the others. Sometimes I lie in bed at night and worry for the whole human race.

"I'm really sorry," I said.

"Where. Were. You. Young. Lady?" my mom asked, doing her one-word-at-a-time voice.

"I was just with Rachel," I said. "And Jake."

My parents exchanged a look. My dad put his hand over his mouth. He was hiding a smile. At the same time, he was trying to look extra stern.

My mom leaned back and put her hands on her hips. "You know we have discussed your dating," she said, "and I thought we decided you were still too young."

"Dating?" I said weakly.

My mom sighed. Then she shook her head. "Maybe it's time for us to have another talk about the birds and the bees."

I swear the blood drained out of my whole head. Then it came rushing back into just my cheeks and neck so that they burned. "Um . . . I'm not dating."

"It's nothing to be ashamed of," my dad said gruffly. "You're a normal young girl, you have certain . . . interests, certain . . . fascinations, a natural . . . curiosity."

At this point I wanted to dig a hole right in the living room floor, crawl in, and pull the rug over me.

"All we're saying is be honest with us," my mom said, all stern again. "Do not make us worry about you."

"Absolutely! I swear! I will never make you worry again! Can I go now?"

I raced from the living room into the kitchen. I wanted to make myself a sandwich, carry it up to my room, and try to do at least some of my homework.

And I really did not want to be subjected to a big talk abut boys. Good grief!

I was just getting the turkey from the refigerator when a thought occurred to me. I tiptoed back to the kitchen door and pressed my ear against it.

"See?" I heard my mother say smugly.

"You were right, as usual," my dad said.

"It's the only way. Let's face it, Cassie works so hard already, what can you do? You can't give her punishment work or make her stay in her room."

"We have a very cool kid."

That kind of gave me a warm feeling. Your parents have to love you. But I felt as if my parents liked me, too. As a person.

"Yes, we do have a cool kid," my mom agreed. "But on those rare occasions when she screws up the only way to really discipline her is to embarrass her."

They both laughed. Hah-hah-hah.

"Next time we can tell her we're going to have

Jake and his parents over to discuss rules for their relationship," my mom said.

More laughter. Hee-hee-hee.

"Or as a backup plan, we could threaten to take her in to Father Banion for a family discussion about intimacy." That was my dad's suggestion.

So much for my warm inner glow. So my parents knew I liked Jake. And they knew that any discussion of that fact would embarrass me to death.

Parents. You can never completely trust them.

I finished making my sandwich and went upstairs. My room was a disaster area. I am not a neat person. I went to my desk, moved some of my junk aside to clear a work space and opened my binder to find my —

Backup plan?

That's the phrase my dad had used. And Visser Three had said it, too.

Backup plan? Why would the Yeerks want a backup plan? After all, they'd penetrated the big secret of Zone 91 and it was a toilet. True, they had not understood what they'd seen, but they obviously knew whatever it was wasn't a Yeerk ship or a weapon.

So why would they still be inter ested?

I shook it off. Who cared now? We'd wasted enough time at Zone 91. I had better things to worry about. Like homework. And the discovery that my parents knew more about me than I wanted them to.

I did some homework and I went to bed. At four o'clock in the morning, I woke up. I sat bolt upright and stared into the darkness.

"So it's a toilet," I cried. "That's not important. It's an *alien* toilet! An alien toilet! That's the point!"

Of course! Even if it *was* just a toilet, it meant the government had proof of life on other planets. Proof that the Yeerks did not want them to have.

The Yeerks were invading Earth. One of the reasons they were getting away with it was that no sensible person would ever believe it. Even if I went on national TV and announced that aliens were invading, who'd ever believe me? Even if I morphed right in front of people, they'd figure it was just some other kind of weirdness.

But if the government came out and said, "Look, we have proof that aliens exist," then people would start listening. People might even be prepared to believe that the Yeerks were among us.

That's why the Yeerks couldn't just forget

about Zone 91. They couldn't allow the government to have any kind of proof of alien life.

There was a backup plan. That's what the visser had said.

And I suddenly had a pretty good suspicion what it was. Tomorrow evening at nineteen hundred hours, The Gardens would be full of people who worked at Zone 91. Just like the sign-up sheet at the base had said.

I was willing to bet the Yeerks would strike then. What better place to grab some key people from Zone 91 and fill their heads with Yeerk slugs?

Well, there were probably plenty of better places, actually. But Visser Three was not known for being patient. And the trip to The Gardens would be his soonest opportunity to strike.

CHAPTER 22

The Gardens is a combination zoo and amusement park. The two sections are separate, of course. Roller coasters and bumper cars on one side of an artificial lagoon, and animal habitats on the other.

I've spent lots of time at the zoo part of The Gardens. I've spent very little time on the rides. I don't like roller coasters.

From the air it all looks smaller than it does from the ground. Down on the ground, walking along the pink-and-green concrete walkways, it seems endless. But from the air in owl morph, you can see how the pathways curve inside each other like a circular maze. You can see the edges of the park and the world beyond The Gardens.

You can see the endless neon golden arches and Best Western hotels and water slides and putt-putt golf courses.

Of course, in owl morph you can even see the mice cowering down inside the dark bushes. In owl morph there isn't much you can't see.

The Gardens at night is two very different halves. Down below us, the tigers were prowling the limits of their wooded, moat-ringed habitat. And the camels were dozing. And the sea lions were huddled together on their blue-painted concrete island. And the monkeys were sleeping and fussing and occasionally picking bugs out of their ears and eating them.

Over in the amusement park, however, it was a flashing neon extravaganza. The Tilt-a-Whirl was a blaze of blue; the merry-go-round was red and yellow; the roller coasters were wild dragons of racing sequential lights.

I saw a flash! It was the log ride. They shoot photographs of the people in the logs as they fall down the final drop. I heard screams of giddy excitement and fake fear.

In addition to having wonderful eyes, owls can hear a mosquito's wings beating from ten feet away. Tobias was not so lucky. He didn't have an owl morph, so he was his usual red-tailed self. Red-tails don't see or fly well at night.

Wait a minute! Flashbulbs at the log ride?

<Hey! There are people down there! There aren't supposed to be people. The people aren't supposed to be here till eight o'clock!>

<If *they're* here, then the Yeerks are here, too,> Rachel said grimly. <What are they doing here? I thought you said the sign-up sheet at the base said eight o'clock!>

<Actually, it said nineteen hundred hours. But that's eight. Right?>

<Uh, *no*,> Marco said. <Oh, man, these guys have been here for an hour already! The Yeerks may have already infested their targets!>

<Are those the right guys down there? Are they Zone Ninety-one guys?> I wondered aloud.

Jake kept his tone carefully neutral, not wanting to make me feel bad. <There are a lot of sort of twenty- and thirty-year-old guys down there with short hair. Definitely a military-looking crowd.>

I had put it all together *very* early that morning. The Gardens occasionally leases out the entire amusement park to private groups. Especially on slow nights like Sundays.

Zone 91 had leased the park for its soldiers and their families. Of course, on the reservation they were not listed as "Zone 91." They were listed as "Gondor Industries."

I'd spent the day researching on the Internet,

just to be totally sure. There was no Gondor Industries. It was a fake corporation. I was totally prepared and proud of myself for being so smart.

Unfortunately, the hour we should have had to prepare was already gone. All because I could not read military time.

<So who's back at Zone Ninety-one guarding the Toilet From Outer Space, I wonder?> Marco asked.

<I'm sure there are still plenty of guys back there,> Jake said, <and in any case, that's not our problem. Our problem is we have zero time to figure out the rest of the Yeerk plan. All we know is that they may be attempting to use this night to infest several members of the Zone Ninety-one force. But where? Where in all this big amusement park would they do it?>

No time! And it was my screwup. *My* screwup. Oh, man, I had totally messed up. Now innocent men and women might be turned into Controllers because of my stupidity!

Think! Where? Where would the Yeerks try it? <Two possible places,> I said. <They need someplace where they can grab people without being seen, right? The log ride is dark inside. Or the House of Horrors Ride. Those are the only two places.>

<Okay. We split up,> Jake said tersely.

<Cassie, you and Marco come with me for the log ride. Rachel, Tobias, and Ax check out the House of Horrors.>

We split into two separate groups. Jake, Marco, and I flew swiftly toward the log ride, me cursing myself the whole time. <How could I have been so dumb?>

<You weren't dumb,> Jake said. <We wouldn't even have known about this if you hadn't figured it out.>

<For future reference, all you have to do is subtract twelve,> Marco said.

<Huh?>

<To translate military time. Just subtract twelve.> Then, as an afterthought he added, <Duh.>

The log ride was made to look like a mountain. Of course it was really just cement and fake bushes, but it was kind of convincing. We landed on top of it.

<Now what?> Marco asked. <We need to get inside. Can we fly in?>

<Yes, but if we're in owl morph we won't be able to do anything much except flap our wings,> Jake pointed out. <We need to get human again.>

We demorphed as fast as we could and a few minutes later we were climbing down the side of the fake cement mountain, wearing our morphing outfits. And no shoes. Fortunately, at The Gardens people dress even more strangely than that. Some people turned to stare, but not for very long.

The lines were short since the only people in the park were a thousand or so people from Zone 91. Some had brought their kids, so we fit in okay, even though most of the people in line were older guys with short hair and neatly trimmed mustaches.

Into the log ride we went. We took a log, me and Jake in the front, Marco behind us, and a man and woman behind him in the last seat.

The log slipped along the water channel toward the chain lift.

"This would be fun if it wasn't a matter of life and death," Marco said. "I love the log ride. Not as good as the coaster, of course. But the big splash at the end is cool."

"That voice!" someone said. "I know that voice!"

I turned around and looked to see who was talking. To my complete horror, I found myself making eye contact with none other than Captain Torrelli, our interrogator from Zone 91. And at just that moment, the log hit the chain lift and engaged with a loud CHUNK!

"You!" the captain said.

Marco turned around. "Uh-oh."

"What?" Jake asked.

CLANKCLANKCLANKCLANKCLANKCLANK!
Up the slope we went, pressed back into our damp seats.

"You are under arrest!" Captain Torreli said.

"Honey, what is going on?" his date asked.

"Yeah, what is going on?" Jake asked me.

"It's the guy from Zone Ninety-one," I whispered in Jake's ear. "He's recognized me and Marco."

"Uh-oh."

"None of you better move!" the captain said.

And at that point we reached the top of the lift. For a second we were poised there. Then the log tipped forward and gravity took over.

"Ahhhhhh!" the captain's date yelled.

"Ahhhhhh!" I yelled because I hate thrill rides.

"You two are *mine*!" the captain yelled.

And down we went.

WHOOOOOOOSH!

Then . . . spuh-LOOOOOSH!

Water everywhere! The log careened along the narrow channel past big fake models of a logging camp dominated by some great big plaster Paul Bunyan thing.

"If the Yeerks are going to strike, they'll do it in the tunnel up ahead," Jake whispered. "It's like a tunnel of love thing. Real dark."

I wanted to ask how he knew about a tunnel of love. But I stuck to business. "Either way, we need to bail out there. Otherwise we'll never lose the captain."

Marco turned back in his seat, draping his arm over the partition between him and the captain. "You know, I don't think you can really arrest us. I mean, you're military police, right? And this is *not* a military base."

The captain glowered. He whipped a cell phone from his jacket pocket and punched in a number. "Hello? Gardens security? This is Captain Torrelli, security code number eight-seven-two-niner-niner. I need —"

"Good work, Marco," Jake said, rolling his eyes.

"This really complicates things," I whispered.

"Here comes the tunnel," Jake said. "Get ready."

The log boat banged through a doorway into total, absolute darkness.

"Now!" Jake hissed.

I stood up. I turned left. Nothing but darkness. I turned right. Just as dark. Not dark like in-your-room dark when you sleep at night. This was dark like you might as well be blind.

I stepped off the boat, trusting everything to luck.

CHAPTER 23

Never trust anything to luck.

My foot didn't touch anything. I tried to pull back, but it was too late. I pitched forward.

"Aaaahhh!"

SPLASH! Water up to my waist! BANG! The side of the channel. "Owww! My head!" I slipped and fell face-first in the water. I felt the current carry me away.

Then Marco's voice: "Ooof! Owww!"

"You kids aren't going to get away that easy!"

PUH-LOOOSH! "Aaarg!"

"Owww!"

"Hey! Watch where you're driving that boat!"

BONK!

A hand grabbed me! I swung a clenched fist.

"Oww! I need that shoulder!" Jake yelled.

"Sorry!"

"You kids stop where you are!"

Suddenly, there were lights! Lights everywhere! I had been swept along in the current back out of the tunnel. I was back in the night air again, gazing up at neon and incandescence.

I stood up. But the current was too strong. It swept my feet out from under me. I fell and floated.

Behind me, another log boat filled with crewcut guys. Between me and that boat, three heads bobbed in the water: Jake, Marco, and a really angry Captain Torrelli.

"Cassie! Climb out!"

"Oh, no, this is insane!" Marco moaned.

"You kids are gonna do time for this, I swear it!" Captain Torrelli yelled.

BUMPBUMPBUMP. SQUUUEELEEEGEEE!

I was scraped along a sharp turn. I tried to grab the lip of the boat channel and pull myself out, but I was too weak and the force of the water was too strong.

What to do? I couldn't morph. There were witnesses. I'd just have to float along until. . .

Until the big huge drop!

"Ahhhhh!" I cried.

"I think Cassie just figured out where we're headed," Marco said.

"Ahhhhh!" I confirmed.

Another sharp turn. BUMPBUMPBUMP! SQUUUUEEEEGEEE!

And then, just a few dozen feet ahead, just ahead of the log boat we had been in, I saw another boat suddenly disappear. And I heard screams. Happy screams. Totally different from my scream.

"Aaaaaahhhhhh!"

I was racing toward a waterfall. And there was nothing I could do to stop it!

"No! No! Noooooo!"

"Oh, man! No! No! Noooooo!"

"This is insaaaaane! Nooooo!"

"I'll get you kids for this! Nooooooo!"

And over the edge we went. I skidded on my butt down a fifty-foot water slide. Which was bad enough. But just a few feet behind me were two guys and an angry man.

And just a few feet farther back was another log boat. A log boat that would squash us all like bugs if it hit us.

Down I fell, screaming the entire way!

BAH-LOOOOSH!

I hit the lagoon and rolled to my left as fast as I could move my waterlogged body. Something hit me, but it wasn't a boat.

"Hah! Cindy Crawford! You think I don't re-

146

member your name? You are under arrest!" Captain Torrelli cried exultantly.

But then he slipped and his head went under the water and I was out of there.

We joined up just outside the exit from the log ride. Three extremely wet, barefoot kids in bike shorts and aerobics suits.

"You know, basically that was fun," Marco said. "If you set aside the whole could-have-been-crushed-by-a-log-boat thing."

Jake squeegeed the water out of his hair. "Okay, so it's not the log ride. No Yeerks there."

"House of Horrors," I agreed. "Definitely the House of Horrors."

We ran for the House of Horrors. But as we ran there came the sound of a not-too-distant voice crying, "Police! Security! Police!"

So we ran faster.

CHAPTER 24

We ran for the House of Horrors, bare wet feet SLAP-SLAP-SLAPPING all the way. It was halfway across the amusement park. I was panting and sweating and holding my sides from the pain by the time we got there.

"Now what?" Marco asked.

"Now we find the others," Jake said.

"But they could be in morph. We don't even know what we're looking for," I pointed out.

"Exactly. And then we have to figure out if the Yeerks are using the House of Horrors to kidnap and infest guys from Zone Ninety-one."

"Even though we don't know if the Yeerks will be plain old human-Controllers or Hork-Bajir or whatever," I said.

"Exactly."

"And in the meantime," I concluded, "we have to avoid getting arrested by an Air Force captain who is frantically trying to protect the Most Secret Place On Earth, where they are hiding an old Andalite toilet."

Marco laughed sardonically. "Does anyone else ever think maybe we've all just lost our minds? You know, like maybe none of this is real and we're escaped lunatics from the local hospital for the hopelessly wacko?"

"Hey, we're saving the world here, Marco," I said.

"That's what all lunatics say."

"Come along, my wacko friends." Jake led the way toward the House of Horrors entrance.

This ride involved cars on tracks as opposed to log boats in water. I was relieved that at least there wasn't any water.

The three of us piled into one of the cars. A fourth person was seated with us. He was a man, maybe thirty years old. He smiled at me.

"Sure this isn't too scary for you kids?"

"No, sir. We're pretty good at handling scary stuff," I said.

"I don't see the others," Jake muttered under his breath as the car lurched away down the track.

"Boo-ah-ah-hah-HAH!" a mechanical skeleton shrieked.

"Beware! Beware all ye who enter here!" a loud, booming recorded voice cried. "Beware the horrors that lie within!"

Then, "Aaaaaarrrggghh!" A mechanical pirate holding his own severed head jerkily waved a sword at us.

A huge snake turned and aimed its cobralike head at us, staring with glittering green eyes.

"Yeah, yeah, big deal," Marco said. "Could this get any faker?"

"Why are you kids so cynical?" the crew-cut man asked.

"We watch too much TV," Marco answered.

The car spun and banged backward through a doorway into the next room of the House of Horrors. In a flash of lightning I saw the car behind us. In it were also four people. Captain Torrelli and three uniformed Gardens security guys.

"What is *with* that guy?" I asked.

"Hey, Captain, havin' fun?" crew cut yelled back to Torrelli.

"Airman Jones!" Torrelli yelled. "Don't let those kids get away!"

"These kids?" Airman Jones asked, pointing at us.

"Yeah. *Those* kids! At least that girl and the boy with the smirk!"

Our car jerked violently back around and we

were being shrieked at by a flight of ghosts passing overhead.

"That Captain Torrelli. What a joker that guy is," I said weakly to Airman Jones.

"Captain Torrelli has never joked in his life," Jones growled. "You kids are gonna have to stay with me till the captain can talk to you."

We passed beneath the flying ghosts. And that's when the ride got weird. Really weird.

See, somehow, whoever had built the ride seemed to have created perfect, life-size replicas of six Hork-Bajir warriors. And standing behind them, also frozen in place, was a creature with the body of a deer, the tail of a scorpion, and a mouthless face. They were all very lifelike. Probably because they were alive.

Visser Three was in the House of Horrors.

"Okay, *now* I'm scared," Marco said.

"Where are Rachel and Tobias and Ax?" Jake asked in a low voice.

"There," I said. I pointed to a frozen, life-size replica of one of the scariest things on Earth: an eight-hundred-pound grizzly bear. The grizzly was on its hind legs, reared up. It was standing perfectly still. Except for the fact that you could see it breathing.

Sitting atop the grizzly bear was a bird. It was too dark to make out the tail feathers, but I could guess what color they were.

And completing this odd tableau, a rattlesnake was coiled around the grizzly bear's upstretched paw.

Rachel and the others must have seen the Yeerks moving into place. They'd gotten there first and were now waiting for the Yeerks to make their move.

The loudspeaker blared. "Nyah-hah-hah-hah! Beware the graveyard ghouls!"

In between the Hork-Bajir, the visser, and my friends the bear, the hawk, and the snake, were really fake-looking tombstones topped with greenish skulls.

"This is the best part of the ride," Jones said. "Those big blade monsters there are really cool!"

I rolled my eyes. My stomach rolled all on its on.

"This is so totally going to turn ugly," Marco said.

CHAPTER 25

Have you ever known something was going to happen right before it did happen? It almost seems like you're psychic. But usually it's just that your brain has put things together and figured something out.

Well, in the split second before everything cut loose, I realized something: Out in the Dry Lands, the visser had talked about having a list of the humans who would be useful. And who would be more useful to the Yeerks than the head of security for Zone 91?

No time to be subtle. "They'll go for Torrelli!" I yelled.

Our car was turned forward and we were past the tableau of Hork-Bajir and Animorphs. But I heard a loud scream and I knew it wasn't one of those giddy, happy, fun-house screams.

Jake leaped from the car. I leaped after him and collided with Marco. The three of us barely missed being cut in two as the car we'd been in slammed through a narrow door.

I fell to my knees. We were on the tableau! We were suddenly a part of the House of Horrors Ride. And that ride had gone totally gruesome.

Six big Hork-Bajir bounded toward Captain Torrelli's car. It had been his scream we'd heard.

One of the uniformed guards raised his gun. Too slow! A hundred times too slow to beat a Hork-Bajir!

SLASH!

The Hork-Bajir swept its wrist blade.

"Aaaaahhhhh! Aaaahhhh! Aaaaahhhh!" the man bellowed in pain.

The Hork-Bajir yanked the guards up out of their seats and literally threw them back into the scenery. Captain Torrelli was alone in the car. But then two Hork-Bajir grabbed him, careful not to injure him, and lifted him up like he was a doll.

And all the while, the stupid loudspeaker was yammering, "Nyah-hah-hah-hah! Beware the graveyard ghouls!"

But Captain Torrelli was not alone.

"RRRRRAAAWWWRRR!" Rachel roared in

her big grizzly bear voice. She flung the rattlesnake straight at the nearest Hork-Bajir.

The snake — Ax in morph — wrapped itself tightly around the alien's neck and sank poisonous fangs deep.

"Tseeeeeer!" Tobias launched himself, talons outstretched, and ripped at the vulnerable eyes of a second Hork-Bajir.

But that still left four of the big, bladed monsters, not to mention the visser himself. And not even Rachel could handle them all. Although she tried. I swear she grinned a bear grin as she swung one frying-pan-sized paw into the head of a Hork-Bajir.

FWUMP! The Hork-Bajir rocked back and fell unconscious.

SHLUMP! He hit the floor.

<The Andalite bandits!> Visser Three cried in thought-speak.

That's what the Yeerks think we are: Andalites. They know whoever we are, we can morph. And they know only Andalites have morphing technology.

<We can't stay and fight,> the visser pouted. <Much as I would enjoy destroying these vermin! We have priorities. Bring the human!>

"We have to morph!" Jake hissed to me and Marco. "Into the shadows! Before the visser gets away!"

I had already started. This was a fight. I needed something powerful. Something extremely dangerous.

"They're taking the captain!" Marco yelled.

"We can't stop them! We need more firepower," Jake yelled. "Morph!"

My morph was already under way. Thick gray fur was sprouting from every inch of my body. My mouth was becoming a muzzle. A muzzle filled with long, sharp teeth.

<I could use some help here!> Rachel called as she knocked another Hork-Bajir into a wall.

The Hork-Bajir Ax had filled with rattlesnake venom was staggering.

But Visser Three and two of the Hork-Bajir had disappeared from view with Captain Torrelli.

"Cool!" a voice squealed. "Now, this part of the ride is excellent!"

To my amazement, people were still passing by on the ride! Every few seconds another carload rattled past, filled with people who must have thought they were watching the most realistic House of Horrors Ride in all history.

"Look! It's a werewolf!" someone said. He pointed. Right at me. Fortunately, we were all three in deep shadows. No one would ever be able to recognize us.

I was just finishing my morph. I had gone, as quickly as I possibly could, from human to wolf.

Rachel was roaring and belowing. Tobias was shrieking and flapping his wings. Ax was looking for another victim. But the fact was, Visser Three had Captain Torrelli. And the visser was gone.

I looked at Jake. He was just completing his tiger morph. I looked at Marco. He was almost all the way into his gorilla morph. I felt my wolf senses turn on. It was a powerful moment. There is nothing on Earth like a wolf's sense of smell. And nothing much like a wolf's sense of hearing.

I could tell exactly, precisely where Captain Torrelli had gone. I could smell every dragging footstep he had taken.

Then, suddenly, the remaining Hork-Bajir warriors bolted. They raced after Visser Three and Captain Torrelli.

<After them!> Jake yelled.

FWAPP! FWAPP! FWAPP! CA-RUNNCH!

Bright lights! Blazing neon! It took a few seconds for me to figure out what had happened. Then I saw: Visser Three had used his Andalite tail to slice through the back wall of the House of Horrors. His Hork-Bajir had knocked the wall down.

Visser Three, his Hork-Bajir, and poor Captain Torrelli were loose on the grounds of The Gardens.

CHAPTER 26

One evil Andalite-Controller and six Hork-Bajir — several of which were staggering from the wounds Rachel, Tobias, and Ax had inflicted — barrelled into the neon night, dragging a helpless Captain Torrelli.

They were pursued by a red-tailed hawk, a tiger, a wolf, a grizzly bear, and a gorilla with a rattlesnake around his neck.

"Help! Help!" Captain Torrelli cried.

<Back to the ship!> Visser Three yelled.

<After them!> Jake yelled.

<This is insane!> Marco cried. <Insane!>

And the band played "Seventy-six Trom-

158

bones" with lots of loud tuba and louder pounding bass drums.

Yes, I said the band. Because, you see, the nightly Gardens Parade of Characters was swinging up the main street. There was a brass band. In fact there were three. There were dance teams. There were clowns. There were floats. And best of all, there were cartoon characters.

Bugs Bunny, Daffy Duck, Tweety Bird, Sylvester, the Tasmanian Devil, and Pepe Le Pew. They were all there in bigger-than-life costumes, dancing amidst a blaze of colored lights that blotted out the stars.

I ran full-out. I was faster than Rachel. I had more endurance than Jake. The Yeerks were moving swiftly, straight toward the parade.

Suddenly, out jumped a Daffy Duck! Right in Visser Three's path. The Yeerk visser snapped his deadly tail. It flew through the air and Daffy's head went rolling across the ground.

<Noooo!> I cried.

The girl wearing the costume stuck her head up and said, "Hey! What's the matter with you?"

<Aaaahhhh!> the visser moaned. <What kind of creature is that?>

He slowed a bit. Just for a few seconds, as he contemplated the weirdness of a creature with a smaller head inside a larger head. And during that hesitation, we caught up.

Jake let loose a roar that seemed to knock the cotton candy right out of children's hands.

"RRRROOOOAAAARRRRR!"

We all charged. I leaped for the throat of the nearest Hork-Bajir with my yellowed teeth bared in a snarl. The Hork-Bajir swung an elbow blade at me but I twisted with unnatural speed. The blade only sliced fur.

The Hork-Bajir couldn't use its blades. I was in too close. All it could do was claw at me, and that wasn't enough.

A vicious battle raged. Rachel and two Hork-Bajir. Jake, sinking his tiger fangs into another Hork-Bajir. Marco, using Ax's snake morph like a bullwhip, snapping him in to bite, yanking him back out.

And Tobias was using all his speed and agility to tear at the visser's vulnerable Andalite stalk eyes.

"Yay!" a voice yelled.

"Cool!" another voice cried.

And then people started applauding wildly. Without even noticing, we had been swept up into the parade. We had become part of the show.

And the people loved it!

I dropped away from my Hork-Bajir. He was

out of the fight. I ran for the Hork-Bajir who was still yanking Captain Torrelli along. He was way out in front, weaving through the parade. Weaving past Bugs Bunny and Yosemite Sam. Barreling rudely through the brass band, which was now playing "You're a Grand Old Flag!"

"Here boy! Here boy!" some kid yelled as I shot past. Like I was a dog.

The crowd grew thick just ahead of me. Too thick for me to see Captain Torrelli. But I could still smell him. I could smell the minuscule traces of scent left by his shoes. I could smell about ten thousand things right then, everything from candy apples to the grease on the bearings of the Ferris wheel to the gel on a punk guy's hair. It was almost too much.

But I focused hard on just one smell: a few floating molecules that said "Torrelli" to my wolf nose. I put my nose down and shouldered through the crowd. People petted me. People bumped into me. I didn't care. My wolf nose was working, and there was no way I was going to lose the captain.

The crowd thinned out. I looked left, right. I saw nothing. But the scent trail led left and my wolf ears picked out one voice among all the thousands of voices, one sound among all the sounds of The Gardens.

"You're connected with those darned kids,

aren't you?" Captain Torrelli demanded angrily of the Hork-Bajir.

I went after him at a full run. There! A Hork-Bajir dragging the captain. The alien brushed aside a child who had rushed over with his mom to have her take his picture with "the monster."

I timed my approach and I fired my wolf haunches. I flew through the air, aiming right for the back of the Hork-Bajir's neck.

"Rrrumpf!"

"Aaaarrrrggghhh!" the alien cried.

Captain Torrelli broke free and ran like his life depended on it. Which it pretty much did.

I relaxed my jaws and dropped to the ground. The Hork-Bajir and I stared balefully at each other for a few seconds. We sized each other up like a couple of boxers in the ring. But then we both saw and heard the visser go rushing past in a clatter of Andalite hooves.

The Hork-Bajir ran to join his commander and suddenly, the Yeerk invasion of The Gardens was over.

A few moments later, the others caught up to me. We watched a pair of Bug fighters rise from the amusement park and streak into the sky.

They had hidden the Bug fighters in plain sight. They'd been parked atop the Alien Adventure Ride.

As the Bug fighters powered away into the

night, I noticed a kid shaking his head disgustedly. "Those aren't what alien spaceships look like," he said.

"That's for sure," his grandfather agreed. "I was taken aboard a spaceship once. The aliens performed medical experiments on me. And their ship was nothing like that."

CHAPTER 27

The official story in the newspaper and on the local TV news was that a group of pranksters had dressed up as monsters and vandalized the House of Horrors.

They had also carried out a mock abduction of an Air Force captain named Torrelli. The captain was only slightly injured.

Captain Torrelli was quoted in the newspaper as saying, "It was those kids! I am looking for three kids named Fox Mulder, Dana Scully, and Cindy Crawford."

The reporter wondered if perhaps Captain Torrelli had been drinking. And when Captain Torrelli was asked what an Air Force officer was doing at a company outing for Gondor Industries, he said, "No comment. Forget I said anything at all. I was obviously mistaken. Nothing happened."

We met up at the barn the next day. Jake, Rachel, Tobias, Ax, Marco, and me. The Animorphs. The six kids who are trying to save the world.

"Just one question," Rachel asked. "Don't you think, in all fairness, in all decency, in all kindness, we should tell Captain Torrelli he's guarding an alien toilet?"

I shook my head. "No, Rachel. That wouldn't be kind at all. He and the others have a meaning to their lives now. Why should we destroy all that and make them feel trivial and foolish?"

"Ooooh, wisdom," Marco mocked gently. "Deep."

"So the Most Secret Place On Earth remains secret," Jake said thoughtfully. "Maybe that is wise."

<The Yeerks will continue to try and penetrate the secret of Zone Ninety-one,> Tobias pointed out.

"Yeah, but the captain will really be on guard now," Jake said.

"Besides, maybe it's all for the good. It will keep them busy, keep the Yeerks from doing anything more dangerous," Rachel said with a laugh. "Everyone needs a project, right? Everyone needs some hopeless cause to pursue. A quest. A mission."

As she said that last part, she was eyeing the hem of my jeans. Then she started shaking her head. "When did you buy those, Cassie, when you were four?" she asked.

"These jeans are fine."

"Yeah, if you're expecting a flood."

"Wait a minute!" I held up my hand. "Isn't this how this whole thing started?"

"Leave Cassie alone," Jake said, laughing. "We're not going to start this all over. No way."

"Except maybe for the horse-racing thing," Marco said. "See, all I'm saying is, we morph racehorses, right? And then we bet —"

And that's when I dumped a bucket of water on Marco's head and we all went home.

Don't miss

ᕐᑎᓰᒧᕐᑎᒍᕼ5 ™

15 The Escape

Erek the Chee used to be Erek this guy I knew from school. But Erek is a lot more than just some guy.

The Chee are a race of androids. They pass as humans by projecting a sort of holographic energy field around themselves that looks human. Erek may look like a kid. But he is older than human history . . .

"Hi, Marco," Erek said. "Hello, Jake."

We didn't exactly rush over to throw our arms around him. We'd seen what happened the one time Erek did go postal. It was hard to forget. Hard to treat someone that powerful like just another kid.

"Hi, Erek, how's it going?" Jake asked.

"Fine. And we know, through our sources, that you have been doing good work against . . . against our mutual acquaintances." He lowered his voice. "I think we'd better have some privacy."

Suddenly, the air around us shimmered. All the noises of the mall were blanked out. And Erek was no longer human. He was a chrome-and-ivory robot, shaped a little like a lean dog, walking erect.

"What did you do?" I asked.

"I extended my hologram out around us all. People walking by are seeing a group of security guards talking. No one will bother or overhear us. . . .

"Rescuing the two free Hork-Bajir was a good thing. They may prove to be the seeds of something very powerful and good. You may have begun the salvation of an entire race."

I shrugged. "We like to keep busy. It's either rescue entire races or play Nintendo."

Erek laughed with his chrome dog's muzzle. Then he was instantly serious again. "I need to talk to you privately, Marco."

"Well, I don't have any secrets from Jake," I said. "I think that's the basis of a good marriage: openness, honesty."

"It's about someone who was once very close to you, Marco."

My heart stopped beating. I knew instantly who he meant. I started to say something, but my first words died on my tongue. I tried again. "My mom?"

Erek glanced at Jake.

"It's okay," Jake said. "I know. I'm the only one who does."

Erek nodded. "Marco, your mother has returned to Earth. She is overseeing some very secret new project. It's being run from Royan Island. Or, to be precise, it's being run from the waters around Royan Island."

I wasn't really hearing what Erek was saying. I was still back on the part about my mom returning to Earth. Jake understood. He took over dealing with Erek.

"What are they doing out there in the ocean?"

"We don't know," Erek said. "But whatever it is, it would have to be huge for Visser One to be overseeing it . . .

"Look, I . . . we weren't sure whether to tell you about this. But we've learned all we can. And I felt Marco had a right to know she was back on Earth. But you guys have to be clear about something. Visser One didn't get to the top of the Yeerk hierarchy by being nice. She is brilliant and dangerous."

Jake looked at me to see how I was reacting.

"You guys think I don't know what Visser One is like?!" I said hotly.

"I know you do," Erek said. "But humans are easily tricked by outer appearances. You judge people by their faces and eyes. The face of Visser One is the face of someone you trust, Marco. But if you Animorphs decide to investigate this thing on Royan Island, you may come up against Visser One directly . . .

"There's one other clue," Erek said. "We have reason to believe that some new species of Controller is at Royan Island. We believe they are called Leerans."

"Thanks, Erek," Jake said.

"Will he be all right?" Erek asked Jake.

I didn't wait to hear Jake's answer. I turned and stepped out of the hologram. I saw a woman's eyes widen in shock. What she had seen was a kid stepping directly out of a casually chatting security guard.

Jake caught up with me a few seconds later.

"Erek didn't mean anything bad. You know that," Jake said. "He just meant —"

"I know what he meant," I snapped. "He meant if it came to crunch time, would I destroy my own mother to protect the mission? That's what he meant."

Jake grabbed my shoulder and turned me around. "And?"

I was still mad. But I knew why I was mad. It wasn't that Erek had insulted me somehow. It was that Erek was right.

"I don't know, Jake," I said. "I don't know."